Ben Backus
and the Quest for
Cosmic Consciousness

Ben Backus
and the Quest for
Cosmic Consciousness

Christopher Bea

To my lovely wife Tess

So Who Am I?

When all the worlds are sleeping
And the moon spills its face
Upon the floors of my home
A billion stars glitter in my ears
And once again I become
The one eternal moment of my life.
Then I venture outdoors
To gaze upon soundless showers of starlight
Jetting out softly from the center of flowers
While the haloed moon hovers above the hill
Like a giant yellow glowworm:
It shows me the way as I wander in cosmic night
Feeling everything is new and all is right.
Eventually I find myself back in bed
Where I watch fluorescent nebulas
Float behind my closed eyes
Until I fall, asleep.

Contents

Ben Backus
and the Quest for
Cosmic Consciousness

1 Ben Appears

I first met Ben in an ordinary way on an ordinary day. I was leaning over to open my mailbox in the lobby of my apartment building when I heard a pleasant voice behind me say, "Expecting anything special?"

I hadn't noticed anyone in the lobby when I came in, so I was a bit startled.

"No, not really," I replied with an uneasy smile.

I turned around and saw him standing next to one of the large, shiny brown plaster lions that guard the stairs leading up to the upper part of the lobby. As still as the lion, he wore a broad, calming smile. His cherubic face was framed by bright white teeth bordered by a margin of red gums.

"You're new here, aren't you?" he asked.

"I just moved in last week."

"Well then, welcome to our compartmentalized villa."

He bounced down the ten arabesque-tiled stairs to the lower part of the lobby, where I stood by the mailboxes. Reaching out his hand, he said, "I'm Ben."

"I'm Michael," I said, shaking his hand. "I'm on the second floor."

"Oh, do you have a view of the street or the building next door?"

"The building," I frowned. "And the fire escape."

"Well at least you get some light," he added cheerfully. "I'm on the first floor in the second apartment right next to Dorothy's apartment."

He pointed up the stairs and across the upper lobby toward the first-floor hallway. Leaning toward me, he raised his eyebrows and lowered his voice. "Isn't she a character?"

"Yes, she certainly is."

"Did she tell you not to flush Kleenex down the toilet?"

"Yes, only toilet paper."

"Something about the plumbing only being able to handle toilet paper. Who knows, she may be right."

"What is that chiffon thing she wears?" I grimaced. "Is it a nightgown or a dress?"

"I don't know," he shrugged. "But she's the apartment manager and collects our rent. I guess that's all she really wants us to know. Well, that and her car accident that gave her that scar on her face."

"Her car accident?"

"Yes, if I remember correctly, she said it happened somewhere in Pacifica. Wherever that is. She says she has property there. That's all I really know. I'm sure she'll manage to bring it up one of the times you hand in your rent. I guess she feels she needs to explain to people how she got her scar."

"Yes, I had noticed it, of course. But I thought it would be impolite to come right out and ask her about it."

"Naturally."

Normally, I would feel ambushed by a stranger's assertive friendliness and try to excuse myself. But I stood rooted to the spot, listening to him. I sensed I knew him. I felt we might have been childhood friends at some point long ago—perhaps a time before I had a strong sense of myself. He might have been a friend from nursery school or kindergarten, someone I had forgotten while growing up. But I also sensed that he was quite a bit older than I was too. Not a generation older, more likely somewhere in between. Like a much older brother.

He's probably in his early thirties, I thought to myself.

"So, what do you do?" he asked with a smile.

"I'm selling personal computers at the moment. Well, not right now—I mean, right now I'm talking to you. But you know what I mean."

He chuckled at my nervousness. Then he locked his eyes on mine.

"Are you happy doing that?"

"Well, it's okay," I stammered. "It's a living for now. But they say it's the start of a whole new industry. Computers are going to change the world. Everyone will own one in the future, and they're going to affect every aspect of our lives."

He kept smiling at me.

"Why? What do you do?" I asked defensively.

"For the time being, exactly what I want to do," he said a little triumphantly.

I swallowed my envy.

"That sounds great. But how are you able to do that? Are you rich?"

"No, no, I'm on summer break. A self-financed sabbatical."

"So you're a teacher."

"Yes. But this summer, I'm doing a bit of time-traveling."

"I'm sorry, what?"

"I'm traveling from my present to my future."

Now I was smiling.

"Okay, you're going to have to explain that to me."

"Happy to," he said confidently. "Well, you know how most of the time we talk to ourselves about the future, and how we say that in the future we'll do exactly what we want to do if only we didn't have to go to work? Well, I'm doing that now."

"So you're saying that you're in your future right now?"

"Yes. I know that must sound confusing, since we are both here in the present right now. All I mean is that I'm not putting it off—I'm done procrastinating. I'm calling my own bluff. This is it. No more *In the future, I'll do it.* I've given myself the time, space, and freedom to do exactly what I want to do—right now. And that's what I'm doing. I'm there. I'm in that future we all talk to ourselves about."

His eyes slid sideways, gazing over my shoulder.

"Or should I say I'm at my future? Prepositions are funny things. I think they're more important than we give them credit for."

His eyes returned to mine.

"Anyway, I guess you could say my present and future have merged. As I said, I've called my own bluff, so to speak. All that time, day after day, saying to myself: *In the future, I'll do what I really want to do. In the future, I'll be the real me. In the future, I'll do what I was really meant to do.*"

"So what is it that you're doing? Now that you're in your future, I mean."

"Well, today? Absolutely nothing, as a matter of fact."

I smothered a laugh.

"Nothing? What do you mean by that?"

"Just what I said. Today I spent the entire day doing nothing—intentionally. Well, not completely nothing. I did mundane things. I dressed, I ate, I went to the bathroom, I brushed my teeth. Things like that. Doing nothing doesn't mean you have to stand still or be a slob. But it turns out that doing nothing is hard work. It takes concentration—a real commitment. So I went through the entire day without really doing anything significant, not really accomplishing anything at all."

"But why would you want to do that? I mean, do nothing like that?"

"Well, when I woke up today, I thought about the French philosopher Jean-Paul Sartre. He wrote a book called *Being and Nothingness.* Have you heard of it?"

"Actually, I have."

"Have you read it?"

"Actually, I haven't."

"It doesn't matter, not many people have. But anyway, I asked myself: Did ol' Jean-Paul really face nothingness? Sure, he thought about it. He thought a lot about it. But did he really engage with it?"

He paused, looking at me a little longer than was normal.

Finally I blurted out, "You're not really asking me, are you?"

"No, no. That's the question. That's the question I asked myself this morning. Did Jean-Paul Sartre really face nothingness? Didn't he just conceptualize it, and think about it, and write about it? So he just faced the *idea* of nothingness, not nothingness itself. So right then and there, I decided the way to really engage with nothingness was to live it, to *be* it—to experience it. But how could a human being go about doing that? It seemed to me one way to experience nothingness was by doing nothing. If meditation is about *stopping* the brain from thinking, thinking, thinking—well then, the best way to experience nothingness was by *doing* nothing, nothing, nothing. Not trying to accomplish anything at all and see what that did to my mind—to my psychology. So that's why I did it."

I glanced out the paned glass door at a car passing on the street, then looked back at him.

"So what did you learn by doing nothing all day?"

He drew in a deep breath and let it out. A satisfied smile appeared on his face.

"What I learned is that doing nothing is hard. We humans are programmed to always be doing something, to be accomplishing something, to be becoming something. But becoming is easy. Just *being* is hard—extremely hard. That's what you'll experience if you force yourself to do nothing and to accomplish nothing. It's really—"

"Sometimes I feel a sense of accomplishment after a bowel movement," I interrupted. "That's accomplishing something, isn't it?"

He stared at me quizzically for a moment, then burst out laughing.

"Nice one! Good one! Okay, *accomplish*, perhaps that's not the right word. How about *achieve*? Just being is hard—extremely hard. That's what you'll experience if you force yourself to do nothing and to achieve nothing."

"I think that's better, because I can't really say I'm proud after a bowel movement. I do feel a sense of accomplishment, though. But I wouldn't say I achieved something. It's definitely not something I'd feel proud of.

Relief, yes. I'd feel relief, but not pride. So yeah, *achievement* is the better word. Seems that way to me, anyway."

"Well," Ben chuckled, "I'm glad we settled that."

He paused, gathering his thoughts.

"Now, where were we? Oh yes, I didn't really achieve anything today. I didn't read one book or one newspaper or watch television. In fact, I don't even have a television set in my apartment. So I really didn't achieve anything at all today. Not like you. You worked today, right? You made some money. So you must feel you achieved something today."

"Well, yes, but not a great achievement, I have to say."

"That's because it's not what you really want to do in life, is it?"

"No, but—"

"Yes, I know. But in the future…

"Yes, well—"

"No, no. I was only going to say that in the future, you will. I can tell that you're the type who really will. There's nothing wrong with doing what you have to do until you can do what you love and what you're meant to do. And in the meantime, if you can find a way to do what you *like* to do, well, that's good, too."

He slowly began to back up toward the stairs.

"Well, feel free to stop by and say hi anytime to check on my progress. You know where I am. But now I really must get back to doing… nothing—ha! ha!"

I think my mouth must have been hanging open, at least slightly. I watched him turn and glide up the stairs to the upper part of the lobby. Then he flowed left, disappearing around the corner.

**

That night, when it was time to go to bed, I crawled into the old Murphy bed I had detached from the wall and crammed into the alcove.

Lying there, I realized I hadn't really been honest with Ben when he asked if I was expecting anything special and I answered, "No, not really."

In fact, I always hoped something would come to me in the mail, that something would surprise me, that salvation would somehow appear: a winning lottery number, or a letter offering me a wonderful job opportunity with a great salary and plenty of free time. Or at least a job doing something that I really wanted to do. Don't they say, "Find the work you love to do, and you won't have to work another day in your life?"

What was I doing with my life? I had graduated with a degree in English, and now I was selling microcomputers for a base salary with a draw in a retail store called Computer Connection in San Francisco's financial district.

I remember what my uncle Frank said when I told him I was majoring in English: "Why are you doing that?" he asked. "You already know English, don't you? You already speak it, don't you?" He was half-joking, but it still stung—and I couldn't think of a clever reply at the time. And now, even more so. I thought I would be a teacher, but there were no teaching jobs. There was no "market" for teachers these days. San Francisco had enough, thank you very much. And who knew when that would change?

Doing nothing. Living in the present. Maybe Ben was right. But I had to work. I had to think of tomorrow. He had a future to go back to from his self-financed "sabbatical" in San Francisco. He wasn't just living in the present. Not really. He had a secure future tucked away in the back of his mind he could return to. Anyway, this living in the present and not thinking about the future—it's not something you could do in all situations. If you were trapped under the ground in a box, I bet the future would become extremely important. You couldn't just lie there living in the present. You'd be scratching and screaming with all your might to get out of there. You'd be engulfed in a panicked insanity, desperate to get out of your present predicament and into the future, where you would escape a dreadful death. That coffin, that claustrophobic torture, all alone in the pitch-black darkness.

Doing nothing? Come to think of it, aren't some people already happy just being, just doing nothing? We call those people lazy, but who are we to call them lazy? Don't they have a right to just be? Who's to say all the people who are obsessed with becoming something—*becoming* and not just *being*—are right? Live and let live. Isn't that the best policy?

Still, I felt there was something wrong with the whole "doing nothing" idea, philosophically speaking. Hadn't Ben accomplished something by doing nothing? Wasn't his doing nothing all day an achievement? And an achievement means you've done something, doesn't it? So there's a contradiction there. He ended up doing *something* by doing *nothing*. Hadn't I found a flaw in his reasoning? Perhaps I'd discovered a philosophical law, or at least a law of logic.

The more I thought about it, the more convoluted and circular it became. Ben could experience "doing nothing" for a specific period of time—as long as he didn't stop to reflect on it. Or he could continue all day doing nothing, just as he claimed. But once he paused to think about what he had achieved, it nullified his doing nothing by turning it into an achievement. And this cast a logical shadow over the entire enterprise. Wasn't it a word puzzle like *deciding not to decide* or *agreeing not to agree*? Or like that James Bond movie *Never Say Never Again*? It was a paradox, wasn't it?

How I wished I could easily make sure it was. If only the computer world were already here like the representative from Apple Computer said it would be one day in the future. A world where we all could just type a question into our personal computers and get the answer instantly. *Every question on earth.* But the future wasn't here yet. I would have to work with what was at hand. I would have to drag out my big dictionary.

I crawled out of bed, turned on the light, and went over to my Big Dic, as I liked to call it. My Big Dic didn't sit on a revolving library bookstand. It lay at the bottom of my homemade bookshelf, constructed out of pine boards and cinder blocks.

I pulled my Big Dic out onto the floor. I turned it up on its spine, put my thumb on the *OP* half-moon cutout, and let it fall open to the O section. I fingered and flipped through the pages until I found the entry for paradox:

paradox (par´ə doks´), n. **1.** a statement or proposition that seems self-contradictory or absurd but in reality expresses a possible truth.
2. a self-contradictory and false proposition.
3. any person, thing, or situation exhibiting an apparently contradictory nature. **4.** an opinion or statement contrary to commonly accepted opinion. [1530-40; < L *paradoxum* < Gk *parádoxon*, n. use

of neut. of *paradoxos* unbelievable, lit., beyond belief.—paradoxical, paradoxal, adj. —paradoxically, adv. —paradoxicalness, paradoxicality, n. —paradoxology, n.

—**Syn. 3**. puzzle, anomaly, riddle.

Ha! Ha! I said it was a word puzzle, and my Big Dic agreed. It listed "puzzle" as one of the synonyms for "paradox." So if Ben's attempt to do nothing wasn't a paradox, then I don't know what is.

Finding this assurance gave me satisfaction. I felt I had achieved something and therefore earned the right to a good night's sleep.

I crawled back into bed. Lying there, I had one last thought. It occurred to me that Ben didn't even bother to check his mailbox while he was there talking with me. But why would he have? There was no name on the mailbox for the second apartment. I was sure of that. That left me wondering why he had come into the lobby in the first place.

In any case, I knew I wanted to see more of him. But for some reason I didn't want to take him up on his offer to check up on him. Somehow, it felt better to just run into him—by chance as it were.

I drifted off.

2 Our Next Meeting

Over the next few days, every time I approached Ben's door—as long as no one was around—I took baby steps, hoping that I would meet him coming out of his apartment. The stairs going up to my apartment on the second floor were right across from his door. Once I reached the stairs and started to climb them, I stopped on each step and counted to ten until I had ascended beyond the view of his door. At that point, I resumed a normal pace and continued on to my own apartment.

I basically followed the same procedure when I was going down the stairs, except that I started counting to ten on the top stair, figuring that if I heard his door open, I could quickly resume a normal pace and catch him coming out.

When more days passed, and since I hadn't had any luck encountering him, I decided to add another delaying tactic. In addition to taking baby steps, I knelt down on one knee, pretending to tie my shoe. I stayed like that for a while, then I stood up, took another baby step, and knelt down on the other knee, pretending to tie my other shoe. Once I eventually reached the stairs, I started to climb them, counting to ten on each step as usual. When I was coming down the stairs and counting to ten on each step, I began the shoe-tying tactic right at the bottom of the stairs, which was almost in front of his apartment door.

But when Saturday came and I still hadn't managed to "accidentally" run into him, I began to feel that I needed to do something more drastic. So, after lunch, I resolved to just go down to his apartment and knock on his door. After all, hadn't he invited me to stop by anytime to say hi and check on his progress?

So it was that I finally found myself standing at his door. But when I raised my hand to knock, the door suddenly flung open to reveal Ben standing before me.

"Hey Michael, what took you so long?" he announced with a big smile. "Come on in."

He left the door open, turned around, and walked back to the sound of a whistling tea kettle. He called out to me over his shoulder.

"Bring that paper with you, will you?"

I stammered out some sort of reply, picked up the paper at my feet, and walked in, closing the door behind me.

He leaned out from his kitchen area and motioned with his head toward two chairs that flanked a table by the window.

"Take a seat over there. I'll get us some tea, and then I'll fill you in on the latest developments."

I walked over and put the paper on the table next to a stack of books. I sat down on one of the chairs and looked out the window onto Judah Street. It was a sunny Saturday in June. People were strolling by on the sidewalk under the window, most likely on their way to the shops on 9th Avenue. I watched as an electric trolleybus and a number of cars rolled by. Then I looked down at the books stacked on the table next to me, studying their titles:

The Portable Jung
The Portable Nietzsche
The World as Will and Representation
World Hypotheses
The Varieties of Religious Experience
The Decline of the West

I called out to Ben who was preparing the tea.

"Have you read all these books?"

"Mostly. I teach philosophy in the Heartland."

"The Heartland?"

"The Midwest."

"But if you've already read them, why did you lug them out here?"

"Those aren't the kind of books you only read once."

He came over to the table, holding a teapot and two cups. He placed one cup in front of me and the other in front of the empty chair.

Then he held the teapot up at an exaggerated height over my cup and smiled as he allowed a thin, glistening column of tea to stream into it. It made an embarrassing gurgle as it filled my cup. Still smiling, he filled his own cup in the same manner. Finally, he placed a cloth on the table between our two cups and set the teapot on it.

"What do you think of that?" he asked, sitting down.

"Quite a performance," I chuckled. "I don't think you lost a single drop."

"It comes with practice," he said with a grin.

I took a sip of the tea.

"Hey, that's really good tea—really delicious!"

"Thank you. It's my own secret recipe."

I drank some more.

"It's fruity—kind of like a warm wine."

"Yes. But let me draw your attention to what just happened here."

His eyes had a happy mania in them, as if he believed he was revealing a great discovery that would change the world. He pointed to the teapot and then to my teacup.

"The tea was in one container, and then it was in another. One place and then another. That's just how our minds work, isn't it? Our ideas are settled, and then, when we think, they break free from one place and find their way into another. And along the way, they're in between, streaming like the tea—"

I looked down into my cup at the light reddish reflection of my face in the tea. I suddenly thought of Narcissus in the Greek myth, who must have seen himself in a similar way simply by looking into a pool of water before there were mirrors. I began to wonder what a person's self-consciousness must have been like before there were mirrors, but I couldn't continue that thought because Ben broke in.

"—and that tea travels from the pot to the cup. What is that, really? That's an association—a related idea, isn't it? That's what thinking is. Now, if we had more cups here— maybe eight, nine or ten—and we poured tea into those cups, we would have more related ideas, wouldn't we? And then if we poured those cups into a new, bigger container, we would have all those related ideas coming together. And when that happens—kablooey! Like a thunderbolt, a realization strikes you and it alters your consciousness. It's a *real*-ization. It's called that because

17

it's real. It *is* reality. Because that idea, that realization, has moved you into a new way of looking at the world."

Ben leaned back in his chair, raised his eyes toward the ceiling, and then brought them back down to me.

"Another way to look at this is chemically. When you're thinking, you're generating a lot of ideas and then, when you mix enough of them, just as with chemistry, you get a reaction and sometimes startling results. After the poof of the explosion, a molecule is created—something new appears. That's what I live for. Those big moments. Not just little ideas—those are fine—but what I want are the transformations. The big ideas. The big breakthroughs. The big realizations that alter a person's consciousness in a big way. I don't know what else there is to live for. It's what makes life worth living, don't you think? Can you think of anything else that makes life worth living?"

"Well I—"

"Marx said, 'The philosophers have hitherto only interpreted the world in various ways. The point, however, is to change it.' Schopenhauer said that each person is a world unto themselves. So yes, I want to change the world, but what I want to change at this point in my life is my own world. Again, can you think of a better reason for living than that?"

He sat there staring at me, waiting for an answer. I thought for a while before I spoke.

"Well, to be honest, sometimes when I'm extremely hungry and I eat a good meal, I feel, at that moment, that life is good and worth living."

Ben blinked a few times.

"Of course, I often have that feeling too. But that can't be your *real* reason for living, can it? Some say Socrates asked, 'Do you eat to live, or live to eat?'"

I slowly repeated the question out loud.

"Do I eat to live… or… live to eat?"

"Yes, that is the question. Yes, you need to eat to live—that's your means for living—but it shouldn't be your *reason* for living. It shouldn't be your main motive or justification for living, should it? Not if you're a human being anyway. If you live to eat, you're making it your *raison d'être*, as the French say. You're making eating your reason for being. But eating is not really why you get up in the morning, is it?"

"But sometimes I think it might be. I sure look forward to my cup of coffee and buttered toast!"

"Okay, let's say you get up and eat. If that's your reason for living, once you have had your coffee and buttered toast, do you go back to bed?"

"No, I usually don't. But I suppose I might, if I had a hangover, or if I was feeling sick."

"Well sure, but normally you stay up. So perhaps you're not just living to eat, then, right?"

"I suppose not."

"So if you're not living to eat, then why *are* you living? What are you living for? Don't you think you should have the answer to that question?"

Again he was waiting for me to answer. I thought for quite a while, feeling a bead of sweat forming above my eyebrow.

"Okay. How about this: I have to get money to buy food, so I guess I'm living to make money."

"Really? But I thought you just agreed that you weren't living to eat—that you were eating to live. That eating was just a means to live. But if you have to get money to get food—which is a means to live—then getting money is just a means to another means. So you're not really living to make money. Making money is not your reason for living, any more than eating is your reason for living. Making money and eating food are just things you have to do to stay alive. You also have to breathe to live, but you're not living to breathe, are you? Breathing is just one of those things you do mostly unconsciously just to stay alive. Eating, breathing, making money—those things don't answer the question: *Why are you living? What are you living for?*"

"Okay, I suppose you're right," I admitted. "I'll have to think some more about that. And sleep on it too, I guess. But tell me this then… what *are* you living for?"

"Me? That's easy. I already told you. I live for ideas and realizations. *Big* realizations, at that."

"Oh right. Sorry. Of course, you just told me that. But when I met you last week you told me that you were time-traveling. What happened to that?"

"Oh, I'm still doing that. I'm still living my future. Things are crystallizing. I'm figuring it out as I go."

"I see."

I glanced down at the stack of books on the table between us.

"So what can you tell me about these books?"

"Quite a bit. Which one should I start with?"

"Well, I already know about Jung and Nietzsche, so how about this one?"

I pointed to *The World as Will and Representation*.

"Okay, but before we get into that one, do you mind telling me what you already know about Nietzsche?"

"Sure. Well, basically that God is dead. That's what Nietzsche's known for, right?"

"Yes, he is. Is there anything else you know about him?"

"Well, that's the main thing, I guess. Why? What else is there to know about him?"

"God is dead is certainly one of Nietzsche's important insights. But for me, Nietzsche had an even greater realization."

"Which is?"

"Metaphysics is a hiding place from life."

"A hiding place from life? I don't think I've ever heard that before."

"With that one insight—that one realization—Nietzsche pulled the rug out from under all thinking that goes beyond the visible, here-and-now world. Nietzsche makes us ask ourselves how many of our ideas about reality, the world, and the afterlife are actually driven by our fear of life. The facts of the visible world can be scary, so we run and hide into an invisible world of ideas. We feel and see our lives creeping toward death, so we create a non-moving, permanent, everlasting world in our minds."

"Okay now, that is a big realization. An earthquake of a thought. If it's true, it changes everything. It makes all philosophical thinking suspect, doesn't it?"

"Yes. I think it was Nietzsche's biggest realization. And I think his statement that God is dead rests on his revolutionary insight that metaphysics is a hiding place from life. With that one breakthrough idea Nietzsche clears the table, so to speak, and brings philosophical thinking back down to earth. To life on this Earth. We are only human beings, advanced primates on this planet, and there are no supernatural powers. There is no God in heaven and there is no great Plan that we are inevitably evolving toward. It's only us. We are alone. Together."

It was my turn to blink a few times.

"I think you're right about that. I feel that sometimes, but I don't think I've ever heard that said so bluntly and simply before. I think it must be hard to live day to day and keep what you just said in the forefront of one's mind."

"Yes, you're right about that. And that's basically what I wanted to point out about Nietzsche. Now, where were we?"

I pointed to *The World as Will and Representation* again.

The World as Will and Representation

"You were going to tell me about this book."

"Right. With that book, the philosopher Arthur Schopenhauer claimed he had solved the riddle of life."

"The riddle of life? What did he mean by that? Did he mean the meaning of life?"

"No, I think he meant—"

Ben raised his arms and tilted his palms upward.

"What's all this? How is it that all of this exists? How is it that everything—you, me, everyone, everything right now—*is*? Schopenhauer's answer—his explanation—was this book: *The World as Will and Representation*."

"So what's his explanation? Do I have to read the entire book to get it?"

"No, you don't," Ben grinned. "I read it, so that means you don't have to. Unless you want to, of course. In the meantime, I can give you the boiled-down version just by making the title a little more understandable."

"Please do."

"By *World* Schopenhauer means the universe. He doesn't just mean our planet Earth, because *world* can refer to the planet we're on, as well as the sun, the moon, and all the stars in the night sky above. In other words, the universe—or existence itself. So now we can think of our title as *The Universe or Existence as Will and Representation*."

"So what does Schopenhauer mean by *Will*?"

"By *Will* he meant the life force in you right now—that power, that urge, that drive, that energy. And as you look at all the movement and energy in the world outside and around you, that is the same energy and movement that is inside you too. Now our title becomes *The Universe or Existence as Energy and Representation*."

"Okay, that just leaves *Representation*. What does he mean by that?"

"I think a good synonym for *representation* in this case is *manifestation*. So now we have *The Universe or Existence as Energy and Manifestation*. Everything we experience in the world is a manifestation of energy. We are also energy, and we experience it in ourselves and outside ourselves too."

Ben raised his hands up again.

"So how is all this possible? It's because, at its base, the universe is energy, and it is energy manifesting itself in various ways and in various forms. And in one of these forms—us—it turns around and looks at itself. We see the energy around us and feel it within us. Inner and outer are one. *The World as Will and Representation. The Universe as Energy and Manifestation*. It's all a unity. It's all one thing. And we're in it and we're part of it. So the riddle of the world—the riddle of existence—is solved."

Ben tilted his head slightly to the side and looked at me quizzically.

"That's another pretty big realization, isn't it?"

"It is, yes, it certainly is. But I think I'll need some time for it to sink in completely."

"Naturally," Ben nodded.

I touched the spine of the *World Hypotheses* book.

World Hypotheses
"In the meantime, tell me about this one."

Ben raised his eyebrows slightly.

"Well, that's another great book. The author, Stephen Pepper, shows that all the different schools of philosophy can be thought of as being different *world hypotheses*. That's because the different schools of philosophy have different metaphysical stances—and a metaphysical stance, or attitude, or perspective, can be thought of as a hypothesis about the world, or about existence itself. Pepper shows that all the different world hypotheses can be boiled down to four basic analogies—four fundamental *root metaphors*. So, from the philosophies of Plato and Aristotle to those of Descartes, Hobbes, Locke, Berkeley, Hume, Kant, Hegel, Dewey, James, and so on—all of them can be explained as being based on, or originating from, one or more of these four basic analogies or root metaphors. You can think of the four root metaphors as keys that unlock the secret underpinnings of the different schools of philosophy."

"So you've already read this book? Does he succeed? Can all the schools of philosophy be reduced to four root metaphors?"

"Well, I've only read this book once, and that's why I brought it with me. As I said before, these aren't the kind of books you only read once—not for me anyway. But to answer your question, I'd say yes. At this stage, it certainly seems to me that all schools of philosophy can be reduced to one or more of Pepper's four basic analogies. That's because most schools of philosophy can be thought of as having a certain attitude or outlook on the world, and these attitudes or outlooks can be seen as being based on metaphors—*root metaphors*. So when I examine a philosophy, I use Pepper's root metaphors as my starting point to gain insight into what the particular philosophy is based on; in other words, what makes it tick, what holds it together."

"So where does Schopenhauer fit in? What root metaphor is his philosophy based on?"

"Good question. But I think it's best if I first tell you about the four root metaphors."

"Yes, please go ahead."

"The four root metaphors are: *Formism*, *Mechanism*, *Contextualism*, and *Organicism*. As Pepper says, these four world hypotheses are well-grounded, rationally tested and widely applicable ways to explain anything in the world— as well as the world itself."

"It sounds like Pepper was a scientist."

"Well, in a sense he was, because he certainly regarded philosophical theories empirically. He tried to make sense of them in light of the facts of our observable world. Okay, let's start with **Formism**. It's named that because it sees the world in terms of forms or categories. All the particular things in the world are put into boxes—or categories or types—based on their similarity. Things in the world are either similar to one another or not. If they are similar, they're put into one kind, class, type, category or box."

"Or buckets?"

"Exactly. If something is not similar to something else, it's put into a different bucket. Or you could say that a thing is a member of a different category, type, or form. Get it?"

"Got it."

"*Similarity* is the basis, the *root metaphor*, for much of the thinking of Plato and Aristotle."

"But wasn't Aristotle known for inventing logic? Logic doesn't boil down to similarity does it?"

"Actually it does because Aristotle's logic was a kind of container logic. You can think of it as bucket logic. Let's take a syllogism, for example. Premise one: *All men are mortal*. Premise two: *All Greeks are men*. Conclusion: *All Greeks are mortal*. That's container logic in action."

"How exactly?"

"Well, *all men are mortal*—so 'men' and 'mortality' are in the same container. Let's call that container A. Now, *Greeks are men*, so they also go into container A. But since mortality is in container A, Greeks must be mortal too. They're in the same bucket—therefore, Greeks are mortal."

I rested my head in my hands and looked down at the table while I thought out loud.

"I do know Plato is known for thinking that Ideas or Forms exist outside the world. So you have a Form of a horse, and the horses we see around us are copies—similar to that eternal Form. So that's why Plato is a formist, is that right?"

"Very good. You've got it. For Plato, Ideas informed the world. But for Aristotle, the world—and the objects in the world—informed our ideas."

"So were only Aristotle and Plato formists?"

"No. The Medieval Scholastics, like St. Thomas Aquinas, were too. And you can also see strains of Formism in modern philosophers because Formism can also be called *Realism*. And in fact Formism—Aristotle's version especially—is just everyday common sense philosophy. Wouldn't you say that most everyone thinks there are objects, tangible things in the world, which exist outside of their own minds and bodies?"

"Well, yes, of course."

"And in our daily life, don't we take these things for granted? Don't we take them as real?"

"Yes." I nodded.

"And as we look around, don't we see different things? But if we are observant, don't we see some things that are similar in some way, at least?"

"Yes, that too."

"Okay, so much for Formism. Now let's talk about **Mechanism**. The root metaphor for Mechanism is the *machine*. For Mechanism, the world is a highly organized machine-like entity. What is a machine? A machine is a thing that has parts, and those parts are related to each other and interact with each other through cause-effect relationships. Take a bike, for example. It's a machine. How does it operate? I'm going to simplify things, but basically when you step on the pedal, you rotate the chain, which rotates the back wheel, which causes the bike to move. You provide the force by stepping down on the pedal. Moving the pedal is one part that causes the chain—another part—to rotate. That rotation causes the back wheel—another part—to spin, which ultimately causes the bike to move. So, with the root metaphor of the machine in mind, the world can be understood by analyzing its phenomena into their 'working parts,' detecting how each part is acted on by other parts, all within a precise antecedent-consequent, or cause-effect, time sequence. And the parts don't have to just be made of metal or wood. A 'part' can be a mammal's heart, the force-cause can be electro-magnetic energy, and the effect can be a pumping action that circulates the blood throughout the body."

"So which philosophers were influenced by the Mechanism root metaphor?"

"Pepper lists a lot of them, and some of them are called *Materialists*. From ancient times, there were the early Pre-Socratic atomists Leucippus and Democritus. The Roman Lucretius was also an atomist. Then, in the Western world, there's Galileo, Descartes, Spinoza, Hobbes, Locke, Berkeley, and Hume. There's also Marx, with his dialectical materialism. Pepper doesn't mention him, but I think Marx was a mechanist philosopher in some ways."

"That's a lot of philosophers. What's next?"

"Next we have **Contextualism**. It's also known as *Pragmatism*. Pepper says the root metaphor for Contextualism is the *historic event*—but not one that is dead and gone. More precisely, it is the event that is alive in its present. So we can also think of the root metaphor for Contextualism as a *live event* with its setting and its changing context. For instance, right now, in this moment you and I are sitting here in this apartment, at this table by this window, talking about these books, while outside traffic is passing in two directions on the street, and people are walking by on the sidewalk, going about their personal business. On top of that, people are dwelling in the apartments above us, in various parts of this building, going about their lives… someone just dropped something upstairs… and do you hear that? Is that someone yelling? So that's the context—both static and fluid, with many different elements connected to one other in a web of relationships and meanings."

"Yes, I can see that."

"Personally, I like to think of the root metaphor for Contextualism as a *scene in a play*. You have the stage and the particular individuals, all in some kind of relationship to one another, within an environment that serves as the background. The scene includes all sorts of specific things that hold meaning for the characters, along with the objects and words they use, or are influenced by either directly or indirectly."

"But how is that Pragmatism exactly? Isn't Pragmatism the philosophy of the practical: the idea that if something works, it's true?"

"Pragmatism is the philosophy of the practical in the sense that pragmatists regard truth as whatever works or whatever proves successful. But Pragmatists couldn't have that view without presupposing a context or environment, could they? A formist examines a particular thing and decides how it is similar to or different from other things. In contrast, a pragmatist considers a thing in its entirety— its history and context—and judges how it functions or works in relation to the other elements in the environment in which it exists."

"How it functions in relation to other things? That sounds a lot like Mechanism with its focus on cause and effect."

"Yes, but Mechanism narrowly focuses on the parts and the function they perform in the whole machine. Their functions are determined by the machine itself. Contextualism, on the other hand, considers more than just cause and effect. It focuses on how agents or things relate, interrelate, or function in relation to one another. That includes cause and effect, but things can relate to each other in other ways too. For instance, these chairs we're sitting on relate to this table, but not in a cause-and-effect way, right? Also, Contextualism is more open-ended than Mechanism. It emphasizes change and novelty in ways the fixed structure of the machine cannot."

"Okay, I get that now. That clarifies it."

"So that just leaves **Organicism**. The root metaphor for Organicism is life itself, the idea of a dynamic, integrated, developing *organism* whose inner nature unfolds over time. For the organicist, every actual event in the world is more or less a concealed organic process. Think of the miracle of a tree. It begins as a small seed, but after multiple transformations, it becomes one of the largest plants on earth. Obviously, that gigantic tree was inherent in the seed. Why not see the whole world that way? Why not see it as following the pattern of a growing organism, with all its integrated organic parts developing and progressing toward a goal—like the magnificence of a growing tree from a tiny seed? Come to think of it, don't most people feel that way about the world? Don't we think or feel consciously or unconsciously that the world is improving, that people are becoming better, and that all of existence is evolving into something greater and grander?"

"We at least hope it is, I guess."

"Now that you mention it, based on the state of the world right now, it's also easy to see why some people could think the opposite—that the world clearly isn't evolving into something better. Still, I think a lot of people, as you say, *hope* that we and all of existence are evolving into something better. And that's more or less the feeling of Organicism. The most famous philosopher inspired by the metaphor of Organicism was Hegel. He saw reality as a *process*—like a tree, it's an ever-changing, developing, and integrated system. But the image of the tree only goes so far with Hegel, because even though the universe—or reality—for Hegel was an ever-changing, developing, integrated whole, he thought of it as a non-material entity."

"So nonphysical—or spiritual?"

"Yes. So if you take a tree as a metaphor for Hegel's Organicism, you need to leave out the wood," Ben said, smiling.

"And the leaves?"

"Sure," Ben chuckled, "the leaves too. Hegel's system was very abstract and removed from actual life to some degree. So, I think an even better way to understand Hegel's Organicism is with the idea of the human mind. Consciousness itself. Our mind, our consciousness, is not material, and it's definitely not static. Isn't it always in process—constantly evolving, developing, growing and realizing new things?"

"There's no denying that."

"And Hegel's dialectics represents that changing process."

"What are dialectics anyway? I've never been sure."

"Dialectics is Hegel's kind of logic. Instead of relying on Aristotelian container logic—with its propositions, sentences, subjects, predicates, p's and q's, and deductive arguments called syllogisms—Hegel followed the flow of our thinking and our judgment-making as it naturally occurs. His logic wasn't the dead logic of textbooks; rather, it was the live, dynamic logic of human consciousness as it reasons. It was the zigzagging path of the human mind as it thinks about things.

"I'm still not sure I understand."

"Well, consider the way the word good entails the word bad. The only way you can understand the word *good*— which is value judgment—is in relation to the word *bad*. Good only has meaning as the opposite of bad, and bad only has meaning as the opposite of good. Good and bad imply each other. Even though they're opposites, they're inherently related to one another. The same goes for inner and outer. You can only know what *inner* means because of its relation to *outer*. So opposites are related to each other and interact with each other in our consciousness as we think and reason. You could say they are in a dialogue with one another. Hence: *dialectics*."

"They say that Marx turned Hegel upside down."

"Actually, it was Marx who said Hegel had turned dialectics upside down, and that he, Marx, needed to turn it right side up so that it was standing on its feet again instead of on its head."

"I guess Marx was a down-to-earth kind of guy."

"Yes, you could say that," Ben chuckled. "Hegel pointed his dialectics upward—toward the immaterial realm, toward the ideas of consciousness, being, and existence. He believed dialectics—the tension between mental opposites—drove history and progress. Marx, however, believed dialectics should be grounded in material life, in nature. For Marx, it was the dialectical tension, contradiction, and conflict between different classes in society over material and economic goods that pushed history forward, not the dialectics of consciousness."

"So if Marx turned Hegel right side up, what does that make him? Marx, I mean. He certainly couldn't be an organicist, could he?"

"Actually, I think Marx was an organicist and a mechanist. Marx was an organicist when he analyzed what he called the superstructure, but he was a mechanist when he described how the base causes the superstructure."

"Superstructure? Base?"

"*Superstructure* is the consciousness—the mindset—of a society at a distinct period in history. This includes the institutions, laws, religion, art, philosophy, and science of the time. *Base* is the economic organization: the means and modes of production at a certain epoch in history. Marx believed that man's consciousness, which included his culture, laws, and institutions, was determined, or caused, in a mechanist way by the economic base of that historical period. So, for example, the Roman economy during its empire phase was based on imperialism and slavery, which caused it to have a particular superstructure. In other words, it shaped certain ideas, laws, institutions, and cultural values that reflected and supported that economic base of imperialism and slavery. You can clearly see the base and superstructure reflected in our own U.S. history with the differences between the North and the South.

Weren't their different attitudes and ideas about slavery a direct result of the fact that the North and the South were based on different economic systems?"

"Sure seems that way."

"Marx was a *dialectical organicist* when he explained the historical changes that occurred in the superstructure. But he was a *cause-and-effect mechanist* when he explained how the base relates to the superstructure. The superstructure of a capitalistic economy can change in a dialectical way. For instance, after a conflict, workers may win the right to strike or get higher wages—but the base hasn't changed. There are still employers and employees."

"This is all a lot to take in."

"I know. So let me summarize and illustrate the four root metaphors with an ordinary event."

"That's a good idea."

"Okay, let's say I ask a girl out and she says no thank you. Let's see how each root metaphor might help me to understand her response. **Formism** explains things in terms of categories, forms, or types. So why did she say no thank you to going out with me? Thinking in a formistic way, I might decide that she's just the stuck-up type. Or, if I can bring myself to look at it from her point of view, perhaps she just decided I wasn't her type. **Mechanism** mainly explains things in terms of causes and effects, things that happen in an antecedent-consequent time sequence. So why did she say no thank you to going out with me? Maybe because someone else asked her out first. **Contextualism** explains things in terms of the larger context. So why did she say no thank you to going out with me? Perhaps because her parents wouldn't allow it, or perhaps because she had something else already planned, and so on. Finally, **Organicism** explains things modeled after the unfolding of the inherent nature of living systems. So, why did she say no thank you to going out with me? Perhaps because she is a young girl and has not yet developed or matured sexually. Okay so, loosely speaking, that's the typological, causal, situational, or teleological way to look at the world—or anything in the world really."

"Well, that really makes the different world hypotheses easier to understand and remember. One question though, which root metaphor, which world hypothesis, do you think underlies Schopenhauer's philosophy?"

"Oh right, you asked me that earlier. I would say Schopenhauer's philosophy was based on Formism. Because it definitely wasn't based on Organicism."

"Why's that?"

"Because Schopenhauer despised the organicist Hegel with a vengeance. He called Hegel a charlatan and said that his philosophy was a lot of mumbo jumbo. But I think the real reason Schopenhauer couldn't stomach Hegel was that he just couldn't understand where Hegel was coming from. And that's simply because the starting point of Hegel's philosophy was grounded in a completely different metaphor than Schopenhauer's. Hegel was an organicist while Schopenhauer was basically a formist."

"So how was Schopenhauer a formist exactly?"

"To begin with Schopenhauer was heavily influenced by the formist philosopher Plato. Many times in his writings Schopenhauer even referred to Plato as the 'divine' Plato. As you know, Plato thought the underlying nature of existence was the *Forms*, while for Schopenhauer it was *Will*. The Forms and the Will are both based on the formist metaphor of similarity and difference. For Plato, all the things we see around us may look different, but each is similar to a perfect Form that exists beyond this physical world in a transcendent realm. For Schopenhauer, all the things that we see around us appear different, but they are really only one single thing underneath, which he said was Will. Or, as we've said, is energy. And isn't that what modern physics tells us? Don't we all believe these days that waves or quantums of energy are what lie beneath the multiplicity of things we see around us?"

"Yes, very good. I understand that now."

I pointed to *The Varieties of Religious Experience*.

The Varieties of Religious Experience

"What can you tell me about this book?"

"Oh, that one. Well, I can't tell you much about it at this point because that's the one book here that I haven't really started reading yet."

Ben pulled the book out from the stack. He opened it to the title page and turned it toward me.

"But I think I should show you what the subtitle of the book is. See, it's *A Study in Human Nature*. That tells you it's not about the different religions in the world, but how religion is a part of our nature as human beings. It's how religion is based on our psychology. So, it's not a sociological study, it's a psychological one."

"I see."

Ben turned the book back around, flipped the page, and glanced at it.

"Another thing I can tell you is that this book was first published in 1902. The author, William James, is considered one of the founders of Pragmatism."

"So he was a contextualist?"

"Yes, he was."

I pointed to *The Decline of the West*.

The Decline of the West

"Okay, how about this last one?"

"That's another great book. If you want to know what time it is, this is the book for you."

I smirked.

"If I want to know what time it is, shouldn't I just look at a clock?"

Ben laughed.

"Of course, what I meant to say is that this book will help you understand the times you live in. The author, Oswald Spengler, argues that there isn't one world history. Instead, there are multiple world histories. The idea that mankind is progressing toward more knowledge, more freedom, and more prosperity is a uniquely Western notion of the world and history. The familiar division of history into a linear sequence—ancient-medieval-modern—is an illusion. It's just an egotistical, Western stereotype that the West projects onto other cultures in the world. But there is no straight line from those cultures to ours. We just like to believe there is. We like to think that mankind has been marching forward through time and that we are leading the way. But 'mankind' is an abstract concept. There's no such thing you can touch. You can only touch men and women who belong to particular peoples and cultures."

"But aren't peoples and cultures abstract concepts too? You can't touch a people or a culture can you?"

"Yes, but you can touch a person who is related to a people or its culture."

"But I can touch a man who is related to—"

"To mankind? Yes. But mankind does not have a history. It has an anthropological evolution just like any other zoological animal, but no history. Spengler's point is that history, true history, applies to a people and their culture. Sure we can say a certain individual has a history, and by that we mean a personal history. But that is not History with a capital H. A personal history consists of the details of a person's life. History with capital H is not about humanity or mankind as a whole, rather it is about certain peoples or cultures. And for Spengler it is especially about high cultures."

"High cultures?"

"Yes, like Egypt, China, India, the West, and so on. Spengler said high cultures can only be understood in an organic way, not in a mechanistic way. Cultures are living entities. They are born, have a youth, a maturity, and then a slow decline. So, in this book, he lays out the forms—the morphology—of these different high cultures and shows how they are similar to and different from one another. Here let me show you."

Ben removed the book from the stack. Opening it to the last part of the book, he unfolded three heavy-weight pages, reading out their titles:

"TABLE I. 'CONTEMPORARY' SPIRITUAL EPOCHS… TABLE II. 'CONTEMPORARY' CULTURAL EPOCHS… TABLE III. 'CONTEMPORARY' POLITICAL EPOCHS."

"Why does he say *contemporary*?"

Ben turned the book with its long, unfolded pages toward me. He pointed to the POLITICAL EPOCHS page.

"See how he put the word 'CONTEMPORARY' in quotes. That's because he's using that word in a special sense. The four high cultures on this POLITICAL EPOCHS page—the Egyptian, Classical, Chinese, and

Western—are not contemporary in chronological time. They are contemporary in their relative times. They correspond to one another in the same organic stages of birth, growth, blossoming, and decay. These cultures have the same political characteristics, the same patterns and features as one another, even though they occurred at different times."

He pointed to the top row on the page.

"So, for instance, the Mycenaean period of Agamemnon in the Classical culture—which means Ancient Greece and Rome—that period corresponds to the Frankish period of Charlemagne in our Western culture."

He pointed further down the page.

"The Classical Ionic period corresponds to our Baroque period. And those same periods, or stages, correspond to the Middle Kingdom in Egyptian culture and the Late Chou period in Chinese culture."

Pointing a little further down, he added, "And Napoleon corresponds to Alexander the Great."

"So what time are we living in now? What does our current time correspond to?" I asked anxiously.

Ben pointed toward the bottom of the page, to a section titled CIVILIZATION.

"Imperial Roman times. Sulla, Domitian, Caesar, Tiberius. We are in the Civilization period—the last, long stage of a culture. It makes sense. Rome was ruled by a predatory oligarchy, and we are too. Our constitution was created by mostly slave-holding oligarchs, wasn't it?"

"Oligarchs?"

"Yes, the propertied elite, and just like in Rome, we common people can usually only vote for personalities, not actual political platforms. Look at our architecture in

Washington D.C.—it's Roman, for god's sake. We claim to be a democracy, but have you ever found the word *democracy* in our constitution?"

"Well, I…"

"So yes, *The Decline of the West* tells you the times we live in, and they are Roman imperial times. Those times marked the decline of Classical high culture, and so they mark our decline as well."

"Well, I have to say, that's certainly a completely different way of looking at the world and the United States."

"The more things change, the more they stay the same."

I must have looked disheartened, because Ben looked at me with a paternal smile.

"I can see this is a lot to take in. But this doesn't mean it's the end of the world. You still have your whole life ahead of you. Just because the culture around you is in decline doesn't mean that you and the universe are too. Nothing's changed since you walked into this apartment this morning. You still have your life, your hopes, and your dreams in front of you. And the opportunities that were waiting for you are still there. None of that's gone away. It's only your time perspective on the world that's changed. And it's good to know what time you're living in, don't you think?

"I guess so."

"Others will go through life being confused by the things that happen, or worse, they won't even notice them, because they're asleep at the wheel—completely oblivious. But you—you will understand. You will be awake and know what's happening."

"Yeah, I'm going to be so wide awake that I won't be able to sleep at night."

Ben laughed.

"You're a funny guy, Michael. But take heart. Spengler may not be right. The historian Arnold J. Toynbee simply dismissed Spengler's point of view by saying that societies are not in fact organisms, but rather groups of human beings socially related to one another. Spengler used the metaphor of the organism to explain cultures and civilizations, and it produced some striking patterns and correlations about the past, but that doesn't mean it has to be absolutely true as we head into the future. Maybe Spengler is wrong, and the U.S. and the West are just beginning. Perhaps we are actually on our way up and are not in decline. Perhaps that golden light on the horizon is a sunrise, not a sunset. Only time will tell."

I could tell Ben was just saying these things to make me feel better, so I felt I should try to change the conversation.

"Yet the Romans were so different from us. Look at their religion. It's nothing like ours. Their religion isn't even religion anymore—it's mythology. Don't get me wrong, I love mythology, especially Greek mythology. And Roman mythology was a lot like Greek mythology, wasn't it?"

"Yes, there were many correspondences. The Greek Zeus was the Roman Jove, and so on," Ben added.

"Still, I have to say, I love all those Greek gods and myths the best."

"I do too. Who's your favorite Greek god?" Ben asked.

"My favorite Greek god? I've never thought about it. Okay, there's Apollo. There's Ares. There's Zeus. I suppose it would have to be Zeus, come to think of it."

"Why Zeus?"

"He got all the ladies, of course! And he had his way with them. Why, who's your favorite?"

"Tell you what," Ben said thoughtfully, "I understand there's a pretty big museum in Golden Gate Park, and it's walking distance from here."

"You mean the de Young."

"That's right. How about we head over there sometime to see if they have a statue of my favorite Greek god?"

"That's a good idea. The park entrance is only three blocks from here," I added.

We agreed on next Saturday for our little outing to the de Young Museum. Ben started talking about the underlying similarities between Rome and the United States again when I suddenly realized I was feeling light-headed.

In the short amount of time since I had entered his apartment, Ben had fed me a constant stream of startling ideas—so much so that I felt I simply couldn't absorb one more word. It was as if the floor had been yanked out from under me and I was standing on a flying carpet—Ben's point of view of life and the world. How was he able to be so calm and sober when I felt so unsteady and uncertain?

I glanced at my watch and quickly excused myself, saying I had a lot of things to do. I thanked him for the tea, repeating how delicious it was.

I stood up, and he did too. He walked me to the door and opened it for me. I felt self-conscious and a little off balance as I walked up the stairs. I furtively glanced back and saw him standing with his arms crossed, leaning in his doorway, looking up at me. His mouth had a sliver of a smile, and there was a gleam in his eyes.

I still felt unsteady and wobbly when I closed the door of my apartment. On top of that, I felt ashamed because I had lied. I didn't have any real plans for the day. There was nothing I really had to do. I didn't need to go to the laundromat until next week. I had plenty of clean socks, underwear, and shirts.

But how about grocery shopping? I stumbled into the kitchen and opened the freezer door. Plenty of TV dinners. I closed the freezer door and opened the refrigerator door. I bent down to scan its contents. Plenty of beer. But what about cream? I shook the Half-and-Half cream carton. More than enough for days of morning coffee. Closing the door, I stepped over and opened the cupboard. Peanut butter and jelly. Bread. Pasta noodles. Jars of marinara sauce. Looked like I had all the essentials. I definitely didn't need to go shopping.

I left the kitchen and shuffled down my little hallway to the living room. I dropped into my easy chair and stared at the blank TV set for a while. Then I began to think about what Spengler said about us living in Roman times. What did it mean that I was living in Roman-American times, after all? History repeats itself and that's all. So we all weren't really going in some grand direction—we were going in circles. That's what happens if you're lost in the wilderness, they say: you end up going in circles. Humanity was also in a forest of time, just going in circles.

I stared into empty space for a while. Then I looked up at the inflatable globe perched precariously on top of my pine bookshelf in the corner. I could see Africa, with its green, yellow, pink, and brown countries, as well as parts of India, China, and Russia. Geologists tell us that the continents are drifting and that long ago, in the deep pre-human, geological past, all the continents were one big island. Now those continents are somewhat separated, but still imperceptibly drifting apart. A snapshot of invisible geological time. And now here I was, too. Who was I? What did it mean that I was here now at this point in time during the drift of the continents? Nothing to those land masses floating on the Earth's oceans. But everything to me.

My mind turned back to Ben and all the other things he had talked about. It was as if I had just attended a semester-long graduate seminar in philosophy in little over an hour. And all that stuff he said about mixing ideas like tea from different teacups into one big container to get big realizations. Hell, a big realization for me was when I could finally remember a name or a word that had escaped me. And all those different theories about the world and reality. The real world for me was that if I didn't go to work at Computer Connection on Monday, and the next day… and the next day… and the next day… and the next day, I wouldn't be able to pay my rent. Dorothy would evict me. That was reality. That was why most people scoff at philosophy and consider it a waste of time. They already know what reality is. They don't need to engage in philosophical discussions about what is real and what isn't. But still, there was also a side of me that liked it.

As I thought more, I realized I hadn't even gotten the chance to tell Ben my thoughts about his doing nothing and how it was all a big paradox. He was so enthusiastic and so full of ideas that he made you forget whatever it was you wanted to say when you were in his presence. And come to think of it, he didn't even have the *Being and Nothingness* book on the table with his other books. If it had been there, I would have remembered to talk to him about his weird attempt to engage with nothingness.

Still, what did my quibbles about his doing nothing matter in the face of his cascade of fascinating ideas? His questions were so thought-provoking. He was so overwhelming. I wished I had had him as a teacher when I was in college. Very few of my teachers had been inspiring. I couldn't think of any that even came close to Ben. Compared to him, they seemed like mere mortals.

Take what he said about Socrates. I was taught that Socrates was known for two things: *Know yourself* and *The unexamined life is not worth living*. But Ben said he was also known for asking: *Do you eat to live, or live to eat?* I had never heard that one before. How I wished I could type that question into a personal computer and find out if Socrates had really said that. But where could I confirm it?

I thought of walking down Irving Street to the Sunset Branch Library on 18th Avenue. What was that, ten blocks or so? Basically a mile? They might have an article on Socrates in one of the encyclopedias there. But would it contain his question about eating to live or living to eat? Would they even have any of Ben's books there? It would be so much easier if I could just type the name of that Pepper guy or Schopenhauer or Spengler into a personal computer to find out more about them and their writings.

It occurred to me that if I was going to go to the library, it would have to be soon, because tomorrow would be Sunday and they would be closed.

I got up and crawled into my bed in the alcove. Ensconced in my little "bedroom," I lay there staring up at the plain, off-white ceiling and thought:

Maybe I should try doing nothing, just like Ben. I could just lie in bed all day looking at the ceiling. That way I wouldn't have lied to him. That way I really would have a lot to do, even though it was a lot of nothing. I wouldn't be a liar because I would be doing his paradoxical doing-nothing-something.

I dozed off. When I woke up, it was after five. I wondered why I had napped so long. Deciding it was mental exhaustion, I got up to watch the five o'clock news. Then I watched the six o'clock news. Then a silly sitcom. Could watching a stupid TV comedy count as doing nothing?

3   A Trip to the Museum

Working at Computer Connection for the week and continually asking prospective customers, "What can I do to earn your business today?" made me look forward to being with Ben, someone I didn't have to try to sell anything to.

However, it was touch and go whether or not I would be able to spend Saturday afternoon with him because on Friday my manager pressured me at the last minute to work at the store on that day. But I stuck to my guns.

"Sorry, I can't. There's a Saturday event at the Church of the Inner Sunset."

"There's no Church of the Inner Sunset," he sneered defiantly.

I answered with my best poker face.

"There is, and I'm one of its new members."

He jingled the change in his pocket. He always seemed to do that when he spoke with me. I'm not sure if he did that with the other salespeople who reported to him.

"I still say there isn't," he growled.

"There is. And I promised to be there. Sorry."

✳✳

Early Saturday afternoon, Ben and I left our apartment building and strolled down 8th Avenue. We crossed Irving Street and continued to the end of the last block where 8th Avenue meets Lincoln Way. Instead of turning left and walking down to the traffic light at 9th Avenue, we waited for a break in the traffic, darted across Lincoln Way, and then followed the sidewalk to the 9th Avenue entrance to Golden Gate Park.

"You know, this is really a wonderful place," Ben remarked.

He swung his arm up toward the trees and the deep blue sky.

"It's amazing that it has all this and museums too!" he added enthusiastically.

"I know, it's a great park."

"I think I'll start coming over here on a daily basis, just to clear my mind. It's wonderful how my thinking changes when I walk. It's so much clearer and calmer. You know, Aristotle's school was a 'walking school.' It was known as the Peripatetic School. *Peripatetikos* in Greek means walking up and down, so the Aristotelian school of philosophers were the walking-up-and-down philosophers. Kind of funny when you think about it that way, don't you think?"

"Yes. Did they have staircases at their school?"

"What? Why would you think that? Oh wait, I see. Ha! Ha! That's funny Michael—staircases so they could walk up and down. No, I believe they had gardens and walkways and colonnades and those sorts of things. That's what they must have walked up and down."

We walked a little more without speaking, and then he broke the silence.

"But you know, at least one thing's for sure, I don't think anyone could call them armchair philosophers, right?"

"Yes, they sure don't sound like they were couch potatoes."

We walked in silence again, and then he began once more.

"You know my thoughts really are more lively and upbeat when I'm walking. Why is that I wonder? I really think those Peripatetics were on to something. Of course, partly it's because I'm out here with the trees and fresh air and all that, but I think it's more than that too. I think it must also be because I'm *doing* something. I'm walking, I'm accomplishing something. I'm getting exercise and my body is getting something done."

"I read somewhere that human beings are built to walk about three miles a day—"

I suddenly stumbled forward.

"Be careful!" Ben exclaimed, catching my arm to stabilize me.

He looked over his shoulder and frowned.

"Oh, that's why. That part of the sidewalk is upraised there. Now where were we? Oh, yes, I've heard that 'three miles a day' thing too. After all, we human beings are creatures. Our bodies are survival machines and early on in our history that meant a lot of walking, hunting, and gathering just to stay alive. Our bodies aren't going to change that fast just because we mostly live in cities these days, now are they?"

"I would think not."

We walked on. When I saw the sign to the Shakespeare Garden I suggested we go that way, since we could easily get to the de Young Museum from there. We turned at the sign and walked through a tree-lined fountain area, then across a smooth-cut lawn. We approached the wall where a bronze bust of Shakespeare sits in a glass enclosure. Three bronze plaques flank each side of the bust, displaying excerpts from Shakespeare's plays. We stood looking down at the bust. Before long, Ben bent down and peered at it through the glass. After a while, he straightened up.

"Do you know what Mark Twain said about the bust of Shakespeare when he saw it in the church in Stratford-upon-Avon in England?"

"I have no idea."

"If I remember correctly, he said the face had something like a deep, deep, deep… subtle, subtle, subtle, expression—of a bladder."

"A bladder?"

"Well, this bust is a decent bronze version of the traditional Shakespeare. But I've seen a photo of the one that Twain was describing, and it looks like something you might find in front of a fortune teller's tent at a carnival. I think it was made out of wood or plaster, and the lower part was painted a pale blue. Really a low quality, tasteless sort of thing. Definitely not something a true master artist would have made. Odd, because you would have thought that the renowned Shakespeare would have deserved something better."

"You would have thought so."

"It's likely that during his lifetime William Shakespeare wasn't actually known for writing the plays. If he had been, don't you think they would have sculpted a finer statue to commemorate him?"

"Yes, of course."

"If I remember correctly, Mark Twain believed that Francis Bacon was very likely the real Shakespeare."

"Is that so?"

"Well, what I mean to say is that Mark Twain thought that Sir Francis Bacon had actually written the famous plays and poems."

"But in that case, who was William Shakespeare?"

"An actor. Mark Twain thought that, and many others also think that he was just an actor."

"Really? What do you think? Do you think Bacon wrote the plays?"

"Could have. Some think it might have also been Christopher Marlowe, but I think it was most likely Edward de Vere, the 17th Earl of Oxford."

"Who was that? I've never heard of him."

"Edward de Vere was an aristocrat who lived during Shakespeare's time. And I think whoever wrote those plays and poems must at least have been an aristocrat."

"Why's that?"

"Just based on the plays, the content of the plays themselves. They're concerned with aristocratic themes and show evidence that they were written by a highly educated person. I think to have written in depth about that society, that class of people, you had to have access to it, which means you had to be a part of it. I suppose the real identity of the author of the plays will always be a mystery. But that he was most likely highly educated and an aristocrat—well, that certainly makes sense to me. And William Shakespeare was no aristocrat. So, no, I don't think he wrote the plays."

"So how did it come about that we think William Shakespeare wrote the plays?"

"Acting and playwriting just wasn't something that aristocrats were permitted to do at that time. It was beneath their station in life. A true aristocrat couldn't come out as an actor or a playwright. It would have been social suicide."

"Really?"

"Think about it. The word *aristocrat* means 'rule of the best.' An aristocrat was supposed to be the best a human being could be—someone of the highest integrity, someone who doesn't lie. But an actor pretends to be someone else. In a sense, an actor is a liar because he's not being his true self, even if he's an aristocrat playing the role of an aristocrat on stage. A true aristocrat must play only one role in life: himself. How could people be sure that an aristocrat who was also an actor wasn't just acting and pretending in public life too? A true aristocrat never pretends. He is always exactly who he is supposed to be. He has to have complete integrity. So, even if an aristocrat wrote plays, he would have to let someone else take the credit. Otherwise, he would be tainted by the world of the theater—the world of lying and pretending."

"So you think Bacon or this de Vere guy let the actor William Shakespeare take the credit.

"Yes."

"Well, that doesn't seem fair."

"No, not to us. But I don't think it mattered to the real Shakespeare."

"I can't understand that. How could he allow his identity to be taken away from him like that?"

"Identity? He still had his identity."

"How can you say that? You're saying that he was an aristocrat, and that he wrote the plays, but he let a mere actor named William Shakespeare get the credit. How is that not giving up his identity to someone else?"

"Because he wasn't giving up his real identity."

"How can that be?"

"Well, if I asked, 'Who are you?' you would most likely answer with your name, correct?"

"Yes, of course."

"But where did that name originally come from? Not from you. It was a name you started hearing in your infancy. It came from the outside. It's a sound that you identified with, that's all. But somehow, you became that name. Didn't you? It fused with you. You internalized it."

"Yes, of course."

"Now think about this: when you first wake up in the morning, do you immediately think of your name?"

"Well, I—"

"No. In those moments, you are virtually nameless. You have no named identity. You are nobody for a few moments until you remember who you are. But how do you go about remember who you are without thinking of your name? I say it's by remembering your purpose—most likely your purpose for the day, what you want to accomplish, or what you plan to do. But your purpose for the day is just one of the many supporting purposes that, when taken together over a lifetime, make up your bigger purpose—your life's goal, your reason for living. Isn't that right?"

"Well, yes, I suppose it is."

"Identity, therefore, is really so much more than a name. Shakespeare, whoever he really was, understood that too.

In *Romeo and Juliet*, he has Juliet reflect on her beloved Romeo: 'What's in a name? That which we call a rose by any other name would smell as sweet.' A smell is invisible, which means it's an intangible quality, but it's still part of the rose. Likewise your character, your purpose, is also invisible. Your name is only part of your story. In fact, it's a very small part of it at that. Your name is just part of your surface identity, your social identity. But you are so much more than your name, your sex, your address, or your parents' names on your birth certificate. Now, there's no denying that your social identity is very important, especially if you're a member of a race or group that is oppressed in your society. But even so, your real identity, your deeper identity, is really not your name or social status. It's your purpose. It's something you must do, something you must live for. That's your true identity. That's who you really are. It's what you—interacting with your genetic makeup and your society—come to realize is your reason for living. It's what you must do to be able to look at yourself in the mirror each day and feel that you are a valuable human being and that you have self-worth. And you know, I think the Peripatetics probably understood that, too. Purpose is actually one of Aristotle's four causes. He called it the final cause."

"The final cause? That sounds a little ominous."

"Oh, I never thought about it that way. But I guess it does sound a little menacing, doesn't it? Like the Final Solution in Nazi Germany? No, the *final cause* just means what something is made for—what its purpose is.

"Go on."

"Well, take a chair, for instance. It has four causes. 'Cause' in this case means the basis or the ground for its existence. If it's made of wood, then the *material cause* of the chair is wood. If it's made of metal, the material cause is metal. The *formal cause* relates to its structure—its form, and sometimes its function. Chairs usually have four legs, a seat, and a back support. The *efficient cause* is who or what made it. For a chair, that would be the carpenter or the factory production line. And then there is the *final cause*—the purpose of the chair."

"Which is something to sit upon."

"Correct. We humans have these causes, too. Our material cause is carbon atoms, as well as other elements and molecules. Our formal cause is our shape. As humans, we have a head, torso, arms, legs, and so on. Our efficient cause is more problematic and debatable. Is it our parents, God, nature, or evolution that made us? Well, you can decide that for yourself. But our final cause is the special one. Because we must each discover our own final cause— our purpose in life. And we must do that for ourselves. And that's your real identity, that's who you really are. It's got very little to do with your name, which was applied to you from the outside. Your real identity is something you generate from within."

"From within."

"Yes. You can test this yourself. Answer the question, 'Who am I?' without using your name. In fact, when you ask that question silently to yourself, you probably don't even think of your name. Sure, you answer with your name when someone asks who you are. But when you ask that question silently to yourself, you're really inquiring about your purpose in life—your destiny—how you can fulfill and justify your life. You're asking why you're alive."

"Yes, I've been doing that quite a bit lately."

"I think we all do that, sometimes without even putting it into words."

Ben paused for a moment, thinking. Then he spoke again.

"Putting it into words. That's a funny thing to say, isn't it?"

"Is it?"

"Yes. Why do we say we are *putting it* into words? As if a thought is an object, an *it*, that we put *into* words? As if words were containers that can hold thoughts?"

He made his hand into a fist and placed it into the claw of his other hand.

"Yeah, I don't know," I said, knitting my eyebrows.

"But that, in fact, is what we're doing when we say we're 'putting it into words,' isn't it?"

"I guess so. But getting back to identity, how can a person find their true identity? Their purpose?"

"That can be confusing sometimes, because in a sense, you have many identities. Each moment of your life is an identity. You are a breather when you breathe, an eater when you eat, a cook when you cook, a walker when you walk, a swimmer when you swim, a lover when you love, a singer when you sing, a sleeper when you sleep, a dreamer when you dream, a thinker when you think, a writer when you write, a dancer when you dance—"

Ben suddenly stopped and laughed.

"Obviously I could go on like this forever, but what I'm trying to say is that in a sense you *are* those things when you're doing them. Any activity is your identity at the moment you're doing it.

"So identity is a doing?"

"Sure, it's an activity, but it's still only your surface identity, unless you've decided to make it your core identity, your purpose in life. Knowing the difference between your surface identity and your true identity is important to know when you're trying to find your purpose in life. Of course, another thing is the future.

"The future?"

"Sure. If your real identity is what you're going to do—what you feel you must do and what you have to work toward—then how can that happen without the future? You define yourself—you identify with what you're going to do, with what you're going to be in the future. And that's why it's so hard to do nothing. Remember when I first met you? That's what I tried to do all day. Believe me, it's hard."

"I remember that very clearly," I said with a smile.

"At the same time, the future can also be your secret enemy. Your traitorous enabler."

"How's that?"

"Instead of working toward achieving something in the future by working at it today, you tell yourself that you will do that or be that *in the future*. And then you live the rest of the day feeling good about yourself. You feel your decision to do it in the future was the doing. But you haven't done anything to deserve that feeling. It's a false sense of self-worth. It's fraudulent."

"So, use the future, but—"

"Don't abuse the future. Don't use it as an excuse to put off fulfilling your purpose."

"In other words, don't procrastinate."

"Yes, that's it. At the same time, if you haven't found your purpose, or your purpose is not firm, you can easily find yourself identifying with others and being willing to accept their identity. Why do you think so many people have their noses in novels or eyes riveted to a television set? Just think about what happens to your identity when you watch a movie. How readily you forget yourself in the actor or actress. You identify with them, don't you?"

"Well, sometimes I guess I sympathize with them, at least."

"Sympathizing with someone is one way of identifying with them. Have you ever recommended a movie to a friend and been surprised to learn that they didn't like it as much as you did?"

"Oh yes, I've had that experience."

"That's often because they didn't identify with the main character, the other characters, or the point of the film, like you did. If you don't like or identify with one or more of the characters, you're probably not going to enjoy the film, no matter how good the plot is."

"Yes, that makes sense."

"We say man is the rational animal, but I think man is also the *identifying animal*. We live and think by identifying with things. We are always searching for things to identify with, whether they be other people, ideas, nature, our work, our car, our clothes, our social class, our god, our race, our nation—and, hopefully, most important of all, our purpose in life. We can't help it. It's our nature as human beings. Aristotle said man is the rational animal, and he was right. But I say man is the also the identifying animal. So many things become clear when you realize that we are as much identifying animals as a rational ones. Probably more so."

"Can you give some examples?"

"Sure. Take politics, for example. World politics and history are much, much easier to understand when you remember that man is the identifying animal. After all, how could wars happen unless people identified with the nation that wants them to go to war? Racism is the same. You can't have it without people identifying with certain groups and excluding others. Our identifying nature explains so many things. Think of love. What is it? It's strong identification, isn't it? When you are in love with someone, you identify with them so deeply that you want to spend the rest of your life with them."

"I would imagine so."

"So, identification is the key to understanding ourselves and our everyday behavior. And it's also the key to understanding our unconscious life."

"In what way?"

"When you dream, who are you? Have you ever thought of your name while you were dreaming?

"No, I can't remember ever doing that."

"When you're dreaming, the real you, the inner you, the core you—has no name. It doesn't need one. Why would it? You only need a name for the outer world."

"So when I'm dreaming, I'm not the surface me—I'm the real me?"

"Yes."

"But what about purpose? Where's my purpose when I'm dreaming?"

"It's there. It's in the unconscious. In your dreams, aren't you always on the move, trying to get somewhere or get away from something? Aren't you always doing something? In your dreams, you have a purpose. In your dreams, the unconscious you is trying to help the conscious you find your purpose, or, if you've already found it, help you fine-tune it or solidify it."

"Everything you've said is very convincing. But I think I'm going to have to sleep on it," I said with an ironic smile.

Ben laughed, then gestured to the bronze bust of Shakespeare behind the glass.

"So, getting back to Shakespeare, I don't think the real Shakespeare cared that an actor named William Shakespeare got the credit for his writings. The real Shakespeare had to write. He had to create and express himself, and by doing so, he fulfilled his purpose. What did he care if someone else got the credit? No more than someone writing under a pseudonym today cares. He knew what he wrote, and I think the people he cared about probably knew, too. His name was merely his surface identity—his social, outer self—not his real identity."

I glanced around at the Shakespeare Garden.

"Yes, I can see that now. You know, I wonder if someday they'll end up renaming this place the De Vere Garden."

"That would certainly make me happy." Ben laughed. "But I don't think we should wait around for that to happen, do you?"

We took the paved path out of the Shakespeare Garden, passing the trees and bushes next to the Steinhart Aquarium. We crossed the smooth pavement of Music Concourse Drive and descended the stairs into the grounds of the Music Concourse, where we wound our way through dwarf trees arrayed like a small army in the sandy soil.

"Do you smell that?" Ben asked. "Someone's cutting the grass."

I glanced toward the other end of the concourse and saw a groundskeeper driving a small green tractor pulling a lawn mower attachment along the concourse's terraced rim. I pointed toward him.

"Look, there's our fragrance-maker over there."

"Oh yes, I see him," Ben said happily. "How I do love that aroma of chopped green grass!"

We strolled up the sloping walkway and into the de Young Museum, where Ben insisted on paying the entrance fee for both of us. When we entered a large, white-walled room filled with modern art and statues, I stepped over and stood by a painting, pointing to the blank space on the wall next to it.

"I wonder if this museum would consider commissioning an artist to paint us standing here, gazing at this painting, and then hanging that painting of us on the wall—right here. What do you think? That's a modern art idea, isn't it? Do you think they would go along with that?"

"Sure, why not?" Ben chuckled.

We walked on. Ben glanced quickly at the displays but did not stop to study any of them. When we entered a room of ancient Greek statues and vases, I heard him utter a barely audible "Aha."

"Did the Greeks have museums?" I asked, glancing around the room at the colorful pitchers, vases, and statues.

"No, museums really didn't come into being until the Renaissance in Europe."

"So where did people go to see all these things? Where were they displayed?"

"Everywhere, I believe. In front of temples and government buildings. Just like today you might see a statue of Abraham Lincoln or George Washington in front of a city hall, or religious figures in front of churches."

"Oh, right. The statues, but not the vases and pitchers."

"Yes, I think the vases and pitchers were created for everyday use in homes and in rituals. I can't imagine why they would have been displayed in public places."

Ben turned his head toward the center of the room.

"There he is," he said softly.

He walked briskly over to a tall statue. I quickly followed and stood beside him. Ben was still as stone, mesmerized by the figure before him.

It was a large sculpture of a smooth-skinned nude young man, standing with his hip bent to the right. He was holding what looked like a baton in his right hand, while his left arm rested on a narrow, waist-high tree stump. A grapevine twisted up the tree trunk, from which bunches of grapes and leaves grew near the top, under his arm. The fingers of his left hand dangled over a bunch of grapes. Two sets of long, curling, braid-like straps of hair dropped down from each side of his head across his shoulders onto his chest. The hair on his head was arranged into thick waves resembling a woman's coiffure. Two small bunches of grapes grew out from the thick, wavy hair above his forehead. On top of his head was some kind of hat or helmet, fashioned from large leaves.

"Dionysus," I said, reading the label at the base of the statue.

"Yes," Ben murmured, "in all his glory."

"He seems effeminate to me. Look at that hairdo."

"Yes, Dionysus was the god of contrasts, opposites, and paradoxes. So, even though he clearly has the male organ, he is feminine at the same time."

"I don't think I've ever heard of him. Was he as important as Apollo and Athena?"

"More so, I believe."

"Then why isn't he as well-known?"

"I'm not really sure. Perhaps it's because his father was Zeus, but his mother was Semele, a mortal woman. So, it's likely he wasn't considered a full-blooded Olympian god, since he was half-mortal."

Ben broke off and began to step around the statue, studying it. He circled back and ended up standing next to me again.

"Do you know how his mother died?"

"No."

"She asked Zeus to present himself in his full splendor—in all his power and glory. When he did, she was vaporized by the burning brilliance of his lightning-bolt essence. That same yearning to see and experience the ultimate power—the true reality of the universe—was in her son as well. That desire to invoke the ultimate and stand face to face with it."

Ben looked around the room, then back at me.

"Did you know that all Greek plays were dedicated to Dionysus and performed in his honor?"

"No, I didn't."

"It was sort of like how the Catholic Mass is conducted in honor of Christ and his Passion story. Dionysus was a unique god because, whereas all the other Greek gods and goddesses acted upon you from the outside, Dionysus acted upon you from the inside. Dionysus possessed you. If the spirit of Dionysus was in you, you were capable of creating something great, such as writing a tragic play that drew back the curtain of ordinary, everyday life to reveal the true reality of existence—life in all its horror and ecstasy."

"Horror and ecstasy? I think I would like the ecstasy part, but not the horror part."

"Me too," Ben confessed with a closed-mouth smile.

"What is meant by the horror part, anyway? I haven't found much horror in life. Sadness. Disappointment. Boredom. Yes. But not horror."

"Oh, horror is there. Life feeds on life. Have you ever watched a nature show that really shows what happens in the wild? How about war? Oh yes, with life, there is horror." He paused. "And ecstasy too, thank God."

At that moment, Ben's face appeared unusually large to me—frozen in time.

I looked back up at the statue.

"Well, in any case, he's just a statue now."

Ben looked startled.

"Oh no! He's still alive. He never really died."

"But Nietzsche said God is dead."

"Yes, he did. That's true. But the god Dionysus is not dead. He's everywhere—in every living thing. As long as there is human life, there will be Dionysus. He represents the life force and the indestructibility of life."

I pointed to the sign at the base of the statue.

"It says here that he was the god of wine."

"That was just one aspect of him. Dionysus shouldn't be reduced to only being the god of wine. More importantly, he is the god of the ecstatic experience—the god of the transcendent experience.

"You know, I've always wondered, what exactly does 'transcendent' mean?"

"Transcendent? Well, etymologically speaking, the word transcendence comes from the Latin prefix *trans-*, which means 'beyond,' and the Latin word *scandere*, which means 'to climb.' So it means to climb beyond, or to go beyond, ordinary experience."

"So a transcendent experience is an extraordinary experience."

"Yes, if you mean *extra-ordinary* in the strict sense of going beyond everyday, ordinary experience. Going beyond normal human limits.

"Okay, so if Dionysus is alive today, how exactly can a person experience him?"

"In plenty of ways. For instance, through your dreams—he's the force behind them. Music is another way. Anytime you listen to music that you like, music that transports you, you are experiencing Dionysus. You are transcending ordinary experience. Music is magical. It possesses you. The notes come into your ears, take hold of you and propel you into an altered state of mind—into a kind of trance. Normally, when you hear ordinary sounds such as conversation, cars on the street, or someone hammering a nail, you don't go into a trance, do you? Your thoughts don't float off into an imaginary world, do they? You don't start humming, tapping your fingers on the table, swaying back and forth, or break out into a dance, do you?"

"Well no, I—"

"And sporting events—Dionysus is there too. When you go to a baseball or football game, you lose yourself in the crowd. You unite with the crowd as you root for your team or one of its players. So, anytime you go beyond yourself—when you 'get out of yourself,'—you are one with Dionysus."

"So, Dionysus is the god of losing one's identity."

"Yes, I guess you could say that. But really, you haven't lost your identity. You've just taken on another identity for a period of time. At that time, your identity is Dionysus."

"That doesn't seem right, based on what you said about identity before and how it is tied in with purpose."

"Remember what I said earlier about how, at any moment, you are what you do. If you're singing, you're a singer; if you're eating, you're an eater; and so on. Taking a break or vacation from your main identity for a time is all right—and can't be helped—because everything you're doing at every moment is an identity. So you can't be your main identity at every moment of your life, can you? Sometimes you just have to be an eater, or a sleeper, or a defecator, or someone in a museum, right? And if, during some of those times, you can become Dionysus, consider yourself lucky. As long as you remember to come back to your true identity—to your purpose—in the end. That's all that matters."

"So, Zeus… Ares… Apollo… I assume none of those is your favorite god. It's Dionysus. Dionysus is your favorite Greek god. Am I right?"

Ben grinned.

"How did you ever guess?"

He glanced around the room, then looked back at me.

"Do you want to explore around here some more?"

"Nah. We already got what we came for. Besides, how could anything beat what we've already seen here?"

We both took one last look at Dionysus. Then we turned and headed out the way we came. As we were walking down the museum's sloping walkway, Ben stopped and pointed across the lawn toward a large, dark, globe-like object. It was located between two sphinxes mounted on granite pedestals.

"What's that?" he said. "Let's see what it is."

"It's either an oil tank or modern art," I joked.

We began to make our way toward it.

"It looks like it could be an old train engine or a gigantic potbelly stove," Ben surmised.

"Yes, it does look like an old potbelly stove," I agreed. "And it seems to be sprinkled with black, sooty, molten blobs of something."

When we reached it, we could clearly see that it was not a potbelly stove nor was it covered with black, sooty, molten blobs. Instead, we beheld an enormous dark bronze vase, voluptuously adorned with a myriad of finely sculpted cupids, cherubs, satyrs, and other animal-like creatures. They were all swarming over grapes, grapevines, and each other in a feverish upward motion toward the narrow neck and mouth at the top of the vase.

I looked down and read the sign at its base:

Gustave Doré created this colossal vase for French winemakers and decorated it with figures associated with the rites of Bacchus, the Roman god of wine. The revelers include cupids, satyrs, and bacchantes, who protect the grape vines from pests.

"Look, it says it was made by Gustave Doré and that he decorated it with figures from the rites of Bacchus, the Roman god of wine."

"Bacchus was the Roman version of Dionysus," Ben said matter-of-factly.

"Oh, right! Kind of amazing that we should run into this just after visiting his counterpart inside the museum, don't you think?"

"Yes, it is. Well, now that we've seen it, shall we go?"

I agreed, sensing that Ben didn't care to discuss the matter any further.

We walked back across the Music Concourse and took the sidewalk along the main street instead of cutting through the Shakespeare Garden. Reaching the exit of the park at 9th Avenue and Lincoln Way, we stood at the curb waiting for the light to change. Suddenly, Ben nudged me. Raising his eyebrows, he motioned with his head to the other side of the street.

A gorgeous young woman wearing light brown shorts and a white, sleeveless blouse stood at the front of a crowd at the curb, waiting for the light to change. Her suntanned legs glowed. Her brown braided hair fell down over her voluptuous breasts. Her bronze face, full red lips, and bright white smile radiated a stunning, aphroditic beauty.

The signal changed, and she began to cross the street, walking toward us. A line of people followed her, as if she were leading an entourage of hangers-on. As she walked by, she smiled at us. But I was too shy to gaze directly into her eyes. When I glanced at Ben, he was staring intently at her, grinning. I looked back to behold her again, but all I could see was the crowd following her.

As we reached the other side of the street, I turned toward Ben and blurted out, "Dionysus?"

"In all his glory!" Ben laughed.

We strolled up the first block of 9th Avenue. Shortly after we crossed Irving Street, Ben stopped abruptly in front of a pay phone. He excused himself, saying he needed to call someone.

I walked on. After a time, I looked back at him. He was smiling into the mouthpiece of the phone.

Later that night, I decided to make myself a healthy meal. After boiling some carrots, I warmed up pasta sauce from a jar and poured it over them. As I sat munching my new concoction, I wondered why it didn't taste as good as I thought it would. Was it the sauce or the carrots? Or were both to blame?

I began to think about my day with Ben. So many ideas came into my head—too many to catch hold of before they disappeared. Shakespeare not really Shakespeare. Man, the identifying animal. Dionysus, the living god. Ben gave me an awful lot to think about. Once again, I wished I could push a button on a computer and see what others had to say about those things. But even if personal computers could do that right now, what good would it do me? I sold them, but there's no way I could afford to buy one.

My thoughts drifted off. I stared deeply into the image of the bright red tomato on the pasta sauce jar for a long time. Finally, I got up and went into the other room. I sat in my chair, gazing into the black screen of the television set.

I wondered if I would ever get to the point where I could stare right into the eyes of a beautiful woman the way Ben did. He was so fearless. He looked right at her without needing to look down or away. What was I afraid of? Perhaps I just needed to have a good opening line? Something like, "Hello, you!" That might be a good one. I could see myself saying that to a beautiful woman, as long as she was smiling and locking eyes with me. Of course, it wouldn't work if I just came up to her and said that without our eyes meeting first. Because if I did that, it would just come off as another slick pickup line. But if I had the courage and the poise and the confidence to stare straight into her eyes without blinking or looking away, then I could say, "Hello, you!" to her, and the encounter could take off from there. That's what I could do. Yes, that's all I would need to do.

After a while I found myself gazing up at the corner of the room where the walls meet the ceiling. I wondered if people in ancient times—such as the Greeks or the Romans—did the same thing. Or even the ancient Egyptians. Did they spend a lot of time staring into the upper corners of their dwellings?

Why did I always end up staring up into the corners of my room? If I did it for too long, I would begin to feel guilty or lazy. Ben was right—it was hard to do nothing. Apparently we humans weren't meant to just *be*. Cats and dogs are happy to just sit, staring out at the world, watching it go by. They can just *be* for long periods of time and not feel guilty about it. Not me, anyway. I got up, brushed my teeth, changed into my pajamas, and climbed into bed.

Sometime during the night, I found myself in a dream. I was sitting near the bronze Aphrodite who had passed by us with her retinue when we were coming home from the de Young. She leaned forward and took my hand. She pulled it up her shiny bronze leg—slowly, all the way up in between her legs. Then she pulled it across her belly, up to her soft, pillowy breasts, and then along her braided hair.

All the while, I could sense her staring at me. But I couldn't bring myself to look into her dark, summoning eyes.

I got up and went into the bathroom.

4 Ben's Purpose

As the week went on, I kept thinking about what Ben had said about purpose during our visit to the museum: that humans either have a purpose or must try to find one. Our purpose for living. Our purpose for being alive. Having a purpose—that's what makes us human. That's what gives our life meaning. Without that, we are lost.

But what about those who have found their purpose, but aren't able to actualize it? What about those who can't seem to make it real and a part of their lives in the present? What about them?

He talked about purpose—that people should have one or find one—but he didn't talk about all the ins and outs of that. Especially how hard it is to *become* your purpose.

Sure, it was easy for him. He was a professor at a university. He had a fulfilling job and a good salary that allowed him to do what he wanted to do.

At different times of the day, while I was at work watching and waiting for my next prospect on the sales floor, variations of this train of thought would play like an audio tape in my mind. Deep down, I knew this line of reasoning was probably based on envy. But I couldn't help myself. Another part of me couldn't help but think there was some justifiable excuse for the resentment I was feeling.

At some point, toward the end of the week, I realized that with all his talk of purpose—how one should have a big purpose, how every day when you wake up you might have little purposes for that day, and how those little daily purposes are wound like strands of a rope into one's big purpose—it struck me that Ben had never actually told me what *his* purpose was. If he had mentioned it, he must have said it so vaguely or indirectly that I couldn't remember it.

So, I made a decision that I would simply ask him, in a polite sort of way, what his purpose in life was. That was only fair. I deserved to know that at least, didn't I?

And so it was Saturday mid-morning that I found myself sitting in an armchair across from his futon, making small talk and asking how things were going with him. He said he was taking walks in Golden Gate Park every day and would likely finish *The Varieties of Religious Experience* in a few days.

That's when I brought up the real reason for my visit.

"You know, when we were in the park last week I forgot to ask you something."

"Oh really, what's that?"

"I forgot to ask you what your purpose is."

"My purpose?"

"Yes."

"Heck, I thought it was obvious—especially after everything I said about it."

"I guess I'm a little dense. I tend to need things spelled out for me."

Ben chuckled a little nervously before continuing.

"Okay, yes, I have a purpose and it's this: I want a big realization. One that transforms my consciousness completely. That desire has been with me for a long time now. For many years, in fact. That's not to say that it was formulated into words, but it was simmering beneath the surface for a long time. Now? It's a rolling boil. It's a constant part of my consciousness—so much so that I think it must be built into my consciousness. That it must be a part of its very structure since it's always on my mind. You could say that my consciousness wants more consciousness. A more expanded consciousness. We know that the universe is expanding, so doesn't it make sense that our consciousness is always expanding too? So yes, my purpose is to have a big realization—to get plugged in and stay plugged in."

"Plugged in? Plugged into what?"

He swung his arm up in an arc toward the ceiling.

"The world, the universe, the cosmos—Aristotle's all-inclusive category of Being itself. I create ideas or discover ideas, and those ideas create sparks for me. But I want to go deeper—to be wired into the main current, the continual fireworks that must be at the center of the universe itself. Sometimes I think there must be something like consciousness at the center of the universe. Don't you?"

"Well, I've never thought about it that way exactly. Not so clearly, anyway."

"So that's why I'm here. This is my summer sabbatical. I've come out here and changed my environment to bring about a big change in my consciousness. I'm here to read, to study, to explore, to think—all in search of a way to bring it about."

He stopped speaking abruptly.

Getting up from the futon, he went over to a shelf against the wall. He picked up a book, opened it, and flipped through a few pages. Then he came back over and handed the opened book to me.

"Here, look at this. This says it all."

In the book was an illustration of a man in a robe, crouching on the ground, poking his head through the sphere of our world to gaze at the wondrous cosmic machinery that lies beyond it. The man's left hand was holding a walking stick, which had also poked through to the realm beyond. The man's right hand had likewise pushed into the cosmic realm, and his fingers were stretched apart in a gesture of surprise.

"Oh yes," I said, "I've seen this picture before. It's not something you forget once you've seen it. It's from the Middle Ages, isn't it?"

"It seems like it might be. But it's not known who created it. For me, the important thing is that it shows that I'm not the only person who feels this way. I think people have been thinking this way about the world and existence for a long time—at least in the Western world, anyway."

"So, how do you think you're going to get there? I mean, how are you going to find that place where you can push your head into that world? So to speak."

"That's a good question. If I knew the answer to that I would have stayed where I was and tried to do it back there."

He pointed to the man in the picture.

"Look at this man. Why does he have a walking stick? It's because he's a traveler—a pilgrim. He's a wanderer, and I think he only found enlightenment after traveling to seek it. So I'm on a pilgrimage of sorts, too."

I could see in Ben's face that he seemed less sure of himself. The confidence that he normally exuded was gone. His eyes didn't pierce mine and hold them like they usually did. Instead, he only glanced at me before looking over my shoulder.

I handed the book back to him.

"You'll get there," I said encouragingly.

He took the book without a word, returned it to the shelf, and then walked over to the table and stood, silently looking out the window. I sensed that he hadn't planned on confiding in me that much, and that he might now be regretting having done so. After all, if he had kept his purpose in life to himself, he wouldn't risk exposing himself to shame and embarrassment if he didn't achieve it. But now someone else in the world knew about his grand goal, and it was someone he barely knew. But perhaps that was for the best, because I was not connected to his circle of friends, relatives, or colleagues. That way, if he failed to achieve his goal, I would be the only person who knew, someone far away from where he lived. Someone who could never tell anyone about it.

Ben was still standing at the table looking out the window. An electric trolleybus braked and then rumbled by, causing a reflection to flash through the apartment. He suddenly turned around and said, "How about some tea?"

I was relieved at the opportunity to drop the subject, especially since it seemed to be making him uncomfortable.

"Sure. Should I move to the table?"

"By all means."

He turned and went into his small kitchen area. I got up, walked over to the table by the window, and sat down.

I watched as he put tea bags into a kettle, filled it with water, placed it on the stove, and turned up the flame. Then he came over to the table.

"What exactly is this tea of yours?" I asked as he sat down. "I mean, what's in it?"

"Oh, just a mixture of different herbal teas."

"No caffeine?"

"Not one drop. No stimulants allowed these days."

"Do you drink beer or wine?"

"No, not these days."

"Doesn't that take all the fun out of life? A little dull at least?"

"Not for me. Not these days anyway."

"That seems odd."

"How so? What's wrong with that?"

"Nothing really, I suppose. It's just that you being so enamored with Dionysus, the god of wine and all, but not drinking any… it's kind of like going to Mass on Sunday and not going to communion, isn't it?"

"Ha! Good one. Well, it's like this: I believe in taking the wine thing metaphorically."

"Metaphorically?"

"Yes. Like the love potion in *Tristan and Isolde*. That's not what caused Tristan and Isolde to proclaim their love for one another. The love between them was always there. The love potion just gave them the courage—or the excuse—to admit it. Same here. The big realization is there. It's waiting for me. I don't need alcohol or a drug or a potion to release it. I just need to find it. And even if I did use an external substance of some sort, how could I trust the outcome? How could I be sure the realization wasn't just a hallucination? Why introduce that variable into the mix, and then be unsure as to whether it caused the experience even in some small way?"

"Sounds reasonable to me. But—"

Ben was looking past me and didn't seem to notice that I had interrupted him. He went on thinking out loud.

"And then become dependent on that? No, that's a vicious circle addicts get themselves into. That's not the kind of realization—the big realization that I'm looking for."

Ben's eyes met mine again.

"It's thought that the followers of Dionysus used wine and other things to reach their realizations. But I don't want to depend on anything other than myself. I want to get there naturally. No psychedelics, no alcohol, no marijuana, no drugs."

"Not even a little help from your friends?" I asked wryly.

"Human friends, yes! Of course!" Ben laughed.

Just then, the tea kettle began to whistle. Ben jumped up and returned to the kitchen. Soon he came back with the teapot and two cups. He placed them on the table and then lifted the teapot up high.

I giggled with expectation.

After my visit with Ben, I had my lunch—a peanut butter and jelly sandwich, an apple, and some potato chips. Then I did my laundry, which took a couple of hours: lugging my laundry bags down to the laundromat, jockeying for the available washing machines, and engaging in the subtle scheming required to get a good dryer. Finally, it was time to fold the clothes, pack them up, and lug them back home.

After that, I walked the half-mile down to the Park and Shop to buy groceries for the week. After selecting everything and checking out, I had to carry two bags of groceries the six blocks back home. They're very long blocks and I was sweating most of the way. I could have just gone to the Stand Bi Market kitty-corner from our building, but that would've cost a lot more.

Back in my apartment, I pulled out the ironing board and ironed my five collared shirts for the week. Then I puttered around the apartment for a while. Before I knew it, it was evening.

I decided I had more than earned the right to have a beer. I like to drink it ice-cold, so I took my beer glass from the cupboard and put it in the freezer. About ten minutes later, I was pouring that cold, golden goodness into my frosty glass. I knew just how to tip the can to get a perfect foamy head that stopped at the brim without overflowing. Smiling with satisfaction, I watched the froth melt into a creamy head.

Ben knew his way around a cup of tea. I knew my way around a glass of beer.

Sitting in my easy chair, I drank it down in seven or eight gulps. When I drink a beer, I force myself to pause for a few minutes between each quaff in order to savor and prolong the experience for as long as I can. The whole affair takes no more than ten minutes. But pausing between each chug—that's the most I can do. I could never become someone who sips a beer. Sipping is for wine. Gulping is for beer. And it has to be ice-cold. The whole point is to flood your entire throat with that cold, amber nourishment—every inch of it, all at once. That's how I like it.

And the whole world seems so good and right to me in those few moments when I'm enjoying my ice-cold beer after a productive day. My only regret is not being able to make the experience last even longer. But that's life. You can't always get what you want.

Once my glass was empty, I sat staring around the room, replaying the events of the day. There was now clean underwear and socks in the drawer, ironed shirts in the closet, and food in both the fridge and the cupboard.

I began thinking about how I started the day with Ben. He had answered my question about his purpose in life. And now I knew. He wanted to get plugged into the universe. Well, why not? If anyone could do that, based on what I already knew about him, he would be the one to do it. But still, quite a purpose.

To get plugged in, to get to the bottom of things. To experience the ultimate. Most people think you can only get to heaven after dying. He wanted to find heaven on earth. Well, more power to him. Maybe those people are wrong. Maybe his way is really the right way.

I began to wonder how doing all those mundane things I had done—my laundry, my shopping, and my ironing— were related to my purpose in life. Weren't they just things a person has to do to survive? Well, maybe not survive exactly, but at least to live decently.

Ben wouldn't drink beer because it would go against his purpose. Well, I definitely wasn't ready for that kind of purpose—at least not if it ruled out one innocent little beer a day.

He said that, like in *Tristan and Isolde*, his purpose was there, and he didn't need a love potion—or a beer—to bring it out. I regretted not asking him more about *Tristan and Isolde*. I'd heard their names before, but that was all. I didn't know their story. I was afraid of coming off as ignorant and uneducated by asking about them. I was sure I couldn't find anything about *Tristan and Isolde* in my Big Dic.

It occurred to me that I should make a list of all the terms and names Ben mentioned. Because I couldn't go running down to the library every time he dropped a name or a term I didn't know, could I? But if I did, it would be good exercise. Then again, didn't I get enough exercise walking to the laundromat and the Park and Shop?

Still, all in all, it had been a good day. I had accomplished what I had set out to do. I had found out Ben's purpose. On top of that, I had done my laundry, shopping, and ironing.

Everything considered, I decided I had earned the right to have one more beer. One more golden, ice-cold beer.

5 The Cosmic Consciousness Book

A few days later, coming home from work, I got off the streetcar at 9th and Irving and walked up 9th Avenue, past its shops and restaurants. As I passed 9th Avenue Books, I heard a voice call out to me from behind. I turned around to see Ben raising a book in the air.

"Michael, look at this!" he shouted triumphantly. "Look at what I've found."

He trotted up to me.

"You're not going to believe it," he cried, handing me the book. "Take a look."

I took the book from him and looked at the cover. The words *COSMIC CONSCIOUSNESS* surrounded a kind of porthole. This circular window looked out into outer space—a black celestial sky of swirling stars spiraling into a small, bright white ball of fused stars. This central area was encircled by a glowing green-red halo.

At the bottom of the book were these words:

THE CLASSIC INVESTIGATION
OF THE DEVELOPMENT OF MAN'S MYSTIC
RELATION TO THE INFINITE

The author's name at the top of the book was Richard Maurice Bucke, M. D.

I looked up at Ben.

"It makes me think of that picture you showed me last week of that guy sticking his head out into the cosmos."

"Of course! That occurred to me, too."

"Is it a new book?"

"No, it's not actually."

I handed the book back to him. He opened it to the copyright page and pointed to the date.

"See, look, it was first published in 1901."

"It's that old? And you've never heard of this book before?"

"No, I hadn't. But it was mentioned toward the end of *The Varieties of Religious Experience*. That was the first time I'd ever heard of it. I knew immediately that I had to get my hands on it. Can you believe it? I just walked out of our apartment building and around the corner to this bookstore, and here and it was waiting for me. This is it! I feel this is it! I've really found what I've been looking for. Listen to some of the names listed in the table of contents: Buddha, Jesus, Paul, Mohammed, Dante, Francis Bacon, William Blake, and Walt Whitman..."

Ben turned the page and continued.

"Moses, Isaiah, Socrates, Pascal, Spinoza, Wordsworth, Emerson, Tennyson, and Thoreau—and there's still more."

"Do you think this book is saying that all those guys attained cosmic consciousness?"

"I think so, I mean, I guess so. Well, I've got to read the book first, but it certainly looks that way."

"So what is cosmic consciousness anyway?"

"Well, like I said, I have to read the book, but I'm hoping it's what I've been saying. It's when your mind reaches that big moment—when everything is clear and you've arrived. It's illumination. It's the breakthrough—just like the guy who stuck his head out of the sphere of this world, so he could see all the cosmic things behind it. How everything's related. It's the big realization. That's what I'm hoping it is, anyway."

We started walking slowly back to our apartment building.

"So, what do you think it would be like to experience cosmic consciousness?" I asked inquisitively.

"I don't know. Maybe it's feeling—and knowing—that you're part of everything? Like experiencing infinity, whether you're looking up at the sky or down at the ground."

"Jesus… Socrates… Buddha… Moses… that's really some company of great, god-like men. Do you think that's what they experienced?"

"I don't know. Maybe. We'll see."

"But do you think you could handle cosmic consciousness? I mean, you're—and they're—"

"Men. Weren't they? Let's not put historical figures on some otherworldly pedestal. Let's not let time turn them into an elite race of divine beings. We must be egalitarian and democratic in every spiritual bone of our body. That's what I say, anyway… because realization isn't limiting, it's *un*-limiting. There are no sky daddies or magical books. No mystical, nonphysical entities like the soul or the spirit exist. Your soul is your own unique self—your ego, your psyche, your individuality, your personality, your consciousness… and your spirit, what's that? Isn't that just your meaning-making? And how do we make meaning, except by realizing things? And isn't everyone capable of that?"

Ben stopped walking, opened the book, and looked at its table of contents.

"Besides, there are plenty of not-so-famous people here. Names I've never heard of before. Like Richard Jefferies and J. William Lloyd, for example. Ever hear of them?"

"No, can't say that I have."

"Neither have I. And there are all kinds of people here who are listed only by their initials. I guess they wanted to remain anonymous for some reason. But see? This book is also about everyday, ordinary people—not just extraordinary ones who made it into the history books."

"I see."

We resumed walking. When we reached our apartment building, Ben was glancing down at the book.

"We're here, Ben," I said. "I'll get the door."

"What?—oh," he said, looking up.

I unlocked the door, and he followed me in, looking up only long enough to climb the stairs to the upper lobby. Then he bent his head back down toward the book.

I started to climb the stairs to my apartment and turned to look at him.

"Well, I hope you enjoy the book."

He looked up.

"What?—Yes, right."

Then he looked back down at the book, fumbling for his key.

When I got into my apartment, I immediately took off my suit and put on my jeans and T-shirt. It's not easy wearing a suit and tie all day. Of course, I loosened my tie on the way home, but that only offered slight relief from the full-body entrapment of formal attire.

I sat in my chair, collecting my thoughts, staring at the blank television screen, then up into the corners of the room. I was happy for Ben. He felt he had made a huge breakthrough in his quest for his big realization, and finally the pieces were falling into place for him. He was searching and he was finding, finally accomplishing what he set out to do. He had good reason to be excited.

It made me wish for some sort of breakthrough, too. I got up and started to pace around my apartment.

Discontent had been simmering in me for a while. I was unhappy at Computer Connection. I wasn't making much money, and there didn't seem to be a clear way to make more. There was the draw, technically a salary. But if you sold a computer and earned a commission, the draw was deducted from that commission. So the commission became a kind of mirage in your mind. It definitely wasn't much of an incentive—not something you could really aim for on or count on. The system felt more like a one-step-forward, two-steps-back kind of thing, leaving you demoralized and feeling like you were always in debt.

And then there was the floor traffic. There wasn't always that much of it. When someone did wander in and managed to slip through the net of some other salesperson on the floor, they ended up being mostly curious types, not always people with a definite problem that a computer was the solution for.

We were taught to sell the store, find out what the customer wanted to accomplish, then sell the computer as the solution. But the curiosity seekers would just suck up your time, picking your brain about this new, mysterious technology. If they didn't have a problem that the computer was a solution for, you were just wasting your time with them. You were just letting them jerk your chain, as we sales types put it.

But still, I had learned a lot in my time at Computer Connection. I had gotten real sales experience under my belt.

I thought back to when I sold my first computer. I was talking to a couple, telling them about the benefits of the machine, when the owner of Computer Connection, Mr. Leuba, came over and stood next to me. I introduced him to the couple and resumed talking about the computer—how it worked and what they could do with it.

"They said they want it," he interrupted.

I blushed and stopped talking. I immediately took his word for it, even though I couldn't remember them saying that. I had been so deep into my nervous sales pitch that I had switched off my listening mode.

I excused myself, left them in his hands, and went down to the basement storeroom to grab the computer, the nine-inch monitor, and two floppy disk drives.

So yes, I had a "track record," as they say. I had made some first-time mistakes, and I had gone on to sell a few more computers. It's true that I was only a retail salesman, but it wasn't as if I was a car salesman. By now, I had more than six months of sales experience—and it was with computers the new, exciting world-changing product that everyone was talking about. That surely added a certain something to my resume.

So yes, wasn't it time for me to move on? Hadn't I learned the fundamentals of being a salesman: how to recognize a real prospect, and how to look for problems that the product I was selling could solve? Why not see if I could sell myself to a big company? Why not move into corporate sales?

"It's time!" I shouted out loud. Yes, it was time to start looking for a better position. A fellow salesman at Computer Connection was always talking about how great a company Gillette was, and how he was going to apply for a job there. Of course, I wouldn't want to sell razors and razor blades, but there were plenty of other big companies out there, Fortune 500 companies as they were called.

What was I waiting for? I decided I would start looking at the Help Wanted ads in the Sunday paper.

With that settled, I plopped back down in my easy chair. It's not knowing what to do—not having a plan—that upsets a person. It's not knowing where you should focus your energies. In short, it's not having a future. Now that I had made a decision about that, I relaxed.

I started to think about Ben again.

To think that there was a book that claimed to hold the key to what connected all the great figures of the world throughout time—anyone who was anyone in world history. Ben had really found something there, if it was true.

I wondered why that book wasn't more commonly known. Why—if it held such deep insights about reality and world-historical figures—wasn't it standard reading in colleges and universities? Why did Ben, who was so educated and well-read, have to stumble across it while reading *The Varieties of Religious Experience*—a book from the early 1900s? They say the Bible is the most-read book in the world. Why wasn't *Cosmic Consciousness*?

But I was getting ahead of myself. I would have to wait for Ben's judgment on the matter, at least until he had finished reading the book.

I was glad I had met him on my way home from work. I was interested in that book and wanted to know if it was truly great—and if so, why it wasn't recognized. I wanted to know what it said about cosmic consciousness, what the experience was like, and who throughout history had achieved it. I wanted to know all these things, but not enough to buy the book and read it myself. Ben was certainly more qualified to do that than I was.

Besides, I had more important things to do, like finding a better job. And more importantly, it was time to put my beer glass in the freezer.

6 Book Report

Days passed, and then a week, and then more days. As I was coming down the stairs to go to work, or going back up the stairs from work, I would glance over at Ben's door and imagine him sitting in his apartment poring over the *Cosmic Consciousness* book, completely absorbed, laser-focused on pursuing his metaphysical quest to find the door that opens to the secrets of the universe.

I, too, was curious about those things, but it was everything to Ben—more like a mania. I certainly didn't want to be the one to knock on his door and interrupt him.

Still, a few days later, coming home from work, I felt enough was enough. Without thinking too much about it, I simply walked up to his door and gave it a few light taps. To my surprise, he opened it with a smile on his face. He actually seemed grateful that I was there. He told me he had finished reading the book and was in the final stages of reviewing it and putting it all together in his mind. We arranged a time for me to come by on Saturday afternoon where he would be able to give me the full report.

So it was that I found myself sitting in the armchair in Ben's apartment on Saturday afternoon, waiting for him to begin. He was sitting on the futon across from me, slowly flipping through the pages of *Cosmic Consciousness*, refreshing his memory and preparing for the presentation. I could see that he had marked many of the pages with a yellow highlighter. After a time, he looked up and began enthusiastically.

"It's such a wonderful book in many ways. The author, Dr. Richard M. Bucke, has really created something remarkable with this book. It's unique. As far as I know, there's no other book in which historical figures who may have experienced a major transformation of consciousness, are identified and brought together in one place. That, for me, is the greatest thing about this book."

With a slight frown, he looked back down at the book.

"But before Bucke gets to the individual cases of cosmic consciousness, he spends a lot of time—roughly the first eighty pages—explaining what he thinks cosmic consciousness is."

"So what is it?" I asked impatiently.

Ben's eyes looked up and away from mine, and then came back.

"He thinks it's a third kind consciousness, a third level of consciousness, and he thinks we humans are evolving toward it."

"We're all evolving toward cosmic consciousness? Well, that's pretty exciting, isn't it?"

"Well, yes, and actually—"

Ben looked down at the book and turned to the title page.

"The subtitle of the book is *A Study in the Evolution of the Human Mind*."

I shifted my weight in the chair and leaned slightly forward as Ben continued.

"Bucke says there are more or less three levels of consciousness. He calls the first level basic consciousness, or *simple consciousness*. Simple consciousness is based on perception and sensations. It's the kind of consciousness we share with animals. That means, like all animals, you're aware of the information from your senses—your sight, hearing, taste, touch, and smell. You see and hear, and are therefore conscious of the things around you. You are also conscious of your own body, as well as the things that affect it. You are aware of all these things, but not as separate objects in your mind that you can think about. So that's the first kind of consciousness—simple consciousness. Just a basic kind of awareness based on sensation."

"That makes *sense* to me." I smirked.

Ben nodded with a smile.

"The next form of consciousness is *self-consciousness*. That's what we humans have—and animals don't. It's what differentiates us from them and makes us human. On top of simple consciousness, we have self-consciousness, which means we know that we are conscious, or put another way, we are conscious of being conscious. Even our own consciousness can become an object of thought. As self-conscious, thinking human beings, we can objectify ourselves and step outside ourselves, as it were."

"But how did self-consciousness come about? How did that happen?"

"Bucke says it happened when we evolved to have language—and with language, you get concepts. Without language and concepts we wouldn't have self-consciousness; we'd just have simple consciousness. So, the source of our self-consciousness is language itself."

"But then how did our language and concepts evolve? How did that happen?"

"This is where Bucke gets speculative, in my opinion. He basically thinks that millions and millions of separate sensations and perceptions built up over generations and impinged on the nerves and ganglia of our brains to a bursting point. Finally, our brains had to adapt. An evolutionary break occurred, and concepts were born as a natural way to manage these billions of sense perceptions."

"Do you think he's right?"

"Who knows? I don't think we really have a clear scientific explanation of how language or concepts came about, even today. Some say that it evolved as a way for us to survive—that we needed language to communicate with each other in order to hunt, farm, and defend ourselves in our natural and often dangerous environments—and for those reasons, language was born. What exactly those steps were on the biological-evolutionary level, I don't think anyone really knows. But the main thing, it seems to me, is that no matter how language and concepts came about, there is an obvious, observable difference between the simple consciousness of animals and the self-consciousness of humans.

"Yes, it's obvious."

"And finally, the third form of consciousness is *cosmic consciousness*. Just as the name implies, the prime characteristic of cosmic consciousness is being aware of the cosmos—of its infinity and of its presence in a very direct way."

"It's so exciting that we could all be evolving toward a higher form of consciousness like that. But what exactly makes him think we're evolving from self-consciousness to cosmic consciousness?"

"He thinks the number of people who have experienced cosmic consciousness is increasing from a small number in ancient times, to a larger number in modern times. In other words, it's becoming more common. He also thinks cosmic consciousness represents a new, burgeoning human faculty."

"Faculty?"

"Yes, faculty or ability. He considers our ability to see colors or appreciate music as biologically hard-wired faculties. He then traces the evolution of those faculties—how they appeared and developed over time—and he thinks cosmic consciousness is following that same pattern."

Ben turned to a highlighted page.

"Here, listen to this: *General vision is enormously old, but the color sense probably only about a thousand generations. Sensibility to sound many millions of years, while the musical sense is now in the act of appearing.*"

"Musical sense is now in the act of appearing? That strikes me as odd. I think I have a strong appreciation of music. Music is everywhere. What does he mean it's in the act of appearing?"

Ben nodded.

"I don't get that either. But remember, this book was published in 1901. Music wasn't as prevalent then. It wasn't on the radio or television, because there was no radio or television to speak of at the time. Then again, they did have orchestras, and people played instruments of all sorts, didn't they? So I don't think his idea that our musical faculty was only then taking off and evolving makes much sense either. And I don't think our musical faculty has made gigantic strides since 1901, just because music is more prevalent now. Sure, it's easier to access music these days, but I'm not sure that means our musical sense—our ability to perceive, to enjoy, and to appreciate music—has changed in any significant way. I think people's ability to appreciate music goes back to ancient times at least and probably even earlier. We know, for instance, that musical chords played a major role in Pythagoras's philosophy, and tribal groups made music, too. So I think it's more likely that our musical faculty has been stable and has always been more or less what it is now. It seems to me that the growing sophistication and complexity of music has more to do with the instruments we've been able to create than with an evolving innate musical faculty."

"Yes, that *sounds* right," I said, smirking again. "Now what does he have to say about our color sense? Do you think he's on stronger ground there?"

Ben flipped through a few pages in the book, scanning his highlights. Then he stopped at a page and looked up.

"Well, it's interesting and perhaps a little more convincing. He says that our perception of different colors has increased and evolved from ancient to modern times. His evidence for this is that ancient writers described only a few colors. For instance, Xenophanes mentioned only three colors of the rainbow: purple, red, and yellow. Aristotle also thought the rainbow had only three colors. Meanwhile, Democritus saw four colors in the world: black, white, red, and yellow. Bucke also asks why the sky and heaven are mentioned more than four hundred times in the Bible, yet they're never described as having a color. He notes the blue of the sky is probably more intense in the

Mediterranean world than anywhere else, yet it is never described as blue in Homer's *Iliad* and *Odyssey*. Homer always talks about the wine-dark sea, but not once does he mention a deep blue sky."

"It looks like Bucke might be onto something there. So I guess 'wine-dark sea' means that they saw the sea as dark red."

Ben glanced down at the book.

"Yes, or maybe purple, since Xenophanes spoke of the three colors of the rainbow as purple, red, and yellow."

Ben flipped a page.

"Bucke also asks why the sky isn't described as blue in the *Rig Veda* of India or the *Zend Avesta* of Persia. He thinks this has to do with the fact that red is at one end of the light spectrum and blue is toward the other. So he believes it's natural that we evolved to see reddish colors first and blue colors later."

Ben flipped another page.

"He also thinks that the large number of people who are color-blind proves that our ability to detect colors is a modern faculty that is still evolving."

"Why's that exactly?"

"Because if our ability to see colors were a fully developed faculty, it would be more widespread in the population and color-blindness would be less common."

"I can *see* that," I smirked again.

Ben smiled paternally.

"Still, I'm no expert in anatomy, biology, or genetics, but isn't it possible—even though we may have evolved to see color—that some people are color blind simply because there was a hiccup in the system, one not directly related to evolution? Sort of like how in a manufacturing process, machines are set up to produce something, but at some point in the process glitches happen and some of the products come out defective? If so, color-blindness would not be atavistic—a leftover from previous times when we were all color-blind—but simply a flaw or byproduct that occurs during the genetic, embryonic, or fetal development of an infant's vision."

"I guess I can *see* that, too."

"Also, Spengler, in his *Decline of the West*, says the color blue *did* appear in the Classical period—that is, in Greek and Roman times—especially in painting by tradesmen and on temple friezes. So, according to Spengler, people *could* see blue at that time. Their use of black, white, red, and yellow on their vases, sculptures, and frescoes reflected their primary worldview, which was close-in, earthy, corporeal, and two- dimensional. The lack of blue in their major works of art was therefore the result of cultural and artistic choices. The color blue was associated with the sky and represented the heavens, transcendence, and infinity. That outlook was foreign to the Classical mind. Vistas and far distances were alien to them, and since the blue of the sky represented that vastness, it did not appear as a major element in their art."

"Well, that's a completely different way of *seeing* things."

Ben nodded and smiled again. He looked down at the book and flipped a page.

"Bucke also thinks our sense of smell, particularly our ability to detect different fragrances, has increased from ancient times to modern times. But I don't think we need to delve into that, do we?"

"Not on my account. And correct me if I'm wrong, but I don't think you find all this theoretical stuff that compelling either. Am I right?"

"Like I said before, the best part of this book is about the people Bucke believes experienced cosmic consciousness. I guess I'm just not interested enough to do the in-depth scientific research into his evolutionary theories to determine whether he's right or wrong. And even if we are all evolving toward cosmic consciousness, that will happen as a species, wouldn't it? So, how many generations would it take before it becomes commonplace? When almost everyone in the human population has it? Am I supposed to just sit around waiting for that to happen?"

He paused, glanced toward the window, then looked back at me.

"Anyway, at first glance I'm skeptical for a few more reasons. For instance, isn't evolution about how creatures physically change in order to adapt and survive in their environment? I don't know how a transforming consciousness leads to a physical adaptation. Is cosmic consciousness going to give me an improved way to survive? Is it going to give me more legs or an eye in the back of my head? So no, I don't think cosmic consciousness is necessarily a new or third level of consciousness. Can't it just be an altered consciousness that results from a profound experience? Isn't it natural to strive toward more knowledge and deeper experiences? Isn't it natural to want a big, clarifying experience—to reach a peak experience of some sort? Does it have to be bound up with evolution to make it worthwhile or justified? Also, I suspect Bucke was motivated to think that cosmic consciousness was involved with evolution because Darwin's theory of evolution was only about forty years old at the time Bucke wrote his own book. Evolution was on everyone's minds. It was still the hot topic intellectually. So it makes sense to me that, when Bucke had his own cosmic consciousness experience, he couldn't help but think that he was also undergoing an evolutionary event."

Bucke

"Bucke experienced cosmic consciousness?"

"Oh yes! He was a fabulous man."

Ben looked down at the book, flipping back some pages to locate and reference his yellow highlights. His eyes scanned the pages as he summarized aloud:

"He grew up on a farm in the backwoods of Canada… He was self-taught… At sixteen he left home to see the world… He traveled widely, especially in the western United States… He worked on farms, railroads, and a steamboat… He even worked as a wagon train driver… At one point he fought for his life against the Shoshone Indians for half a day in Utah… Then he mined for gold in California… Unfortunately, that's where he got frostbite. He was caught in a winter storm and ended up losing one foot and half of the other… By then he was twenty-one years old. At that point he returned home, studied medicine, and eventually became a psychiatrist… Later on he became the head of an insane asylum in Canada where he introduced many reforms in procedures. And then—*In 1882 he became Professor of Mental and Nervous Diseases at Western University in London, Ontario. In 1888 he was elected President of the Psychological Section of the British Medical Association, and in 1890 President of the American Medico-Psychological Association.*"

"How old was he when he died?"

Ben turned a page.

"He died in 1902. So let's see, he was born in 1837, and he died the year after this book was published, which was 1901. So 1902…sixty plus three, plus two. He was 65."

"How did he die?"

Ben looked down at the book and read:

"*February 19, 1902, after coming home with his wife from an evening spent at a friend's house, Bucke stepped out on the veranda before going to bed to have another look at the stars, which, as it happened, that night were exceptionally brilliant in the clear winter sky, slipped on a patch of ice, struck his head violently against a veranda pillar, and dropped. He was taken up dead.*"

Ben stopped reading. After a few moments, feeling clever, I broke the silence.

"Who knew focusing on the cosmos could be so deadly."

A shadow passed over Ben's features. He chuckled a little nervously, then turned several pages forward in the book.

"Here's what Bucke says about his cosmic consciousness experience. He tells it in the third person: *It was in the early spring, at the beginning of his thirty-sixth year. He and two friends had spent the evening reading Wordsworth, Shelley, Keats, Browning, and especially Whitman. They parted at midnight, and he had a long drive in a hansom (it was in an English city). His mind, deeply under the influence of the ideas, images and emotions called up by the reading and talk of the evening, was calm and peaceful. He was in a state of quiet, almost passive enjoyment. All at once, without warning of any kind, he found himself wrapped around as it were by a flame-colored cloud. For an instant he thought of fire, some sudden conflagration in the great city; the next, he knew that the light was within himself. Directly afterwards came upon him a sense of exultation, of immense joyousness accompanied or immediately followed by an intellectual illumination quite impossible to describe. Into his brain streamed one momentary lightning-flash of the Brahmic Splendor which has ever since lightened his life; upon his heart fell one drop of Brahmic Bliss, leaving thence forward for always an aftertaste of heaven. Among other things he did not come to believe, he saw and knew that the Cosmos is not dead matter but a living Presence, that the soul of man is immortal, that the universe is so built and ordered that without any peradventure all things work together for the good of each and all, that the foundation principle of the world is what we call love and that the happiness of every one is in the long run absolutely certain. He claims that he learned more within the few seconds during which the illumination lasted than in previous months or even years of study, and that he learned much that no study could ever have taught."*

Ben stopped reading and looked up at me.

"Okay, now that's something, that's really something." I said enthusiastically. "That's really amazing. But why does he say 'among other things he did not come to believe' when he said he saw and knew that the cosmos is not dead matter but rather a living presence, and that man's soul is immortal? Why would he say 'he did *not* come to believe'?"

A slight, pinched frown appeared at the corner of Ben's mouth.

"I know. I wondered about that too and had to re-read it a few times to make sense of it. But if we change the word 'come' to 'need,' I think it becomes clearer. So then we have: *Among other things he did not* need *to believe, because he saw and knew that the Cosmos is not dead matter but a living Presence.* In other words, he didn't *need* to believe those things because he saw and knew those things, he *experienced* those things."

"Yes, that makes more sense. In any case, it was definitely a beautiful and powerful experience. Do the others in the book describe their experience that way?"

"We'll see about that."

"How does Bucke go about deciding the people in his book experienced cosmic consciousness?"

"That's a little confusing in my opinion."

Ben flipped back a few pages in the book.

"On page three he says: *The prime characteristic of cosmic consciousness is, as the name implies, a consciousness of the cosmos, that is, of the life and order of the universe... Along with the consciousness of the cosmos there occurs an intellectual enlightenment or illumination... To this is added a state of moral exaltation, an indescribable feeling of elevation, elation, and joyousness, and a quickening of the moral sense... With these come, what may be called a sense of immortality, a consciousness of eternal life, not a conviction that he shall have this, but the consciousness that he has it already.*

Ben flipped several pages forward in the book.

"But then on page 79 he says: *It will be well to state here (partly in recapitulation) for the benefit of the reader of the next two parts, briefly and explicitly, the marks of the Cosmic Sense. They are:*

a. The subjective light.
b. The moral elevation.
c. The intellectual illumination.
d. The sense of immortality.
e. The loss of the fear of death.
f. The loss of the sense of sin.
g. The suddenness, instantaneousness, of the awakening.
h. The previous character of the man—intellectual, moral, and physical.
i. The age of illumination.
j. The added charm to the personality so that men and women are always (?) strongly attracted to the person.
k. The transfiguration of the subject of the change as seen by others when the cosmic sense is actually present."

"He's added a lot of things there, hasn't he?"

"He sure has. And I have a problem with many of the things he's added because they don't reflect his own experience of cosmic consciousness. For instance, he doesn't even list consciousness of the cosmos as one of his marks—or characteristics—of the experience of cosmic consciousness. Yet he said earlier in the book on page three that that was the *prime* characteristic of this kind of mystical experience. On top of that, it's the title of the book itself for God's sake!"

Ben closed the book and showed me the front cover.

"Yes, I can see that. It's written right there: *Cosmic Consciousness. The Classic Investigation of the Development of Man's Mystic Relation to the Infinite.*"

Ben lowered the book to his lap.

"Well, suffice it to say, that as we go through the individuals he presents in the next two parts of this book I will be looking especially for evidence of consciousness of the cosmos, which is cosmic consciousness itself. In addition to that, I'll be looking for intellectual illumination, joyousness or ecstasy, and a sense of immortality or the eternal—all the things that Bucke himself experienced."

"Who are the individuals again?"

"There are two parts of the book where he identifies people he believes experienced cosmic consciousness—or came close to experiencing it. In the first part, he lists 14 individuals he considers actual cases of cosmic consciousness. In the next part, he names 36 individuals he's less certain about."

Who are the 14?"

Ben lifted the book from his lap and turned to the table of contents.

"Gautama the Buddha, Jesus the Christ, Paul, Plotinus, Mohammed, Dante, Bartolome Las Casa, John Yepes, Francis Bacon—"

"Francis Bacon!" I blurted out. "You mean the man who could have been Shakespeare?"

"Yes, but actually, Bucke thinks Francis Bacon *was* Shakespeare."

"Really? What do you think?"

Ben smiled.

"Let's wait until we get to him. Now the rest of the list consists of: Jacob Behmen, William Blake, Honoré de Balzac, Walt Whitman, and Edward Carpenter. So while it might be expected that Bucke would think religious individuals like the Buddha, Jesus, St. Paul and Mohammed had cosmic consciousness, the surprising thing is that he also thinks literary people like Dante,

Francis Bacon, William Blake, Walt Whitman, and Balzac had it too.

"So, not just religious figures, but writers too?"

"Exactly. But let's start with the first one on Bucke's list, Gautama the Buddha."

Gautama the Buddha

Ben turned to the section on Gautama the Buddha and began to read:

"Siddhartha Gautama was born of wealthy parents (his father being rather a great landowner than a king, as he is sometimes stated to have been), between the years 562 and 552 B.C. It seems sufficiently certain that he was a case of Cosmic Consciousness, although, on account of the remoteness of his era, details of proof may be somewhat lacking. He was married very young. Ten years afterwards his only son, Rahula, was born. Shortly after Rahula's birth, Gautama, being then in his twenty-ninth year, suddenly abandoned his home to devote himself entirely to the study of religion and philosophy. He seems to have been a very earnest-minded man who, realizing keenly the miseries of the human race, desired above all things to do something to abolish, or at least lessen, them. The orthodox manner of attaining to holiness in Gautama's age and land was through fasting and penance, and for six years he practiced extreme self-mortification. He gained extraordinary fame, for which he cared nothing, but did not gain the mental peace nor the secret of human happiness, for which he strove. Seeing that that course was vain and led to nothing, he abandoned asceticism and shortly afterwards, at about the age of thirty-five, attained illumination under the celebrated Bo tree."

Ben turned a few pages.

"Here's Bucke's conclusion to the Gautama section: *Gautama, then, was a case of Cosmic Consciousness, and the central doctrine in his system, Nirvana, was the doctrine of Cosmic Sense. The whole of Buddhism is simply this: There is a mental state so happy, so glorious, that all the rest of life is worthless compared to it, a pearl of great price to buy which a wise man willingly sells all that he has; this state can be achieved. The object of all Buddhist literature is to convey some idea of this state and to guide aspirants into this glorious country, which is literally the Kingdom of God.* So, we can see here that Bucke equates illumination with cosmic consciousness, and he also equates Nirvana with cosmic consciousness."

"I know Bucke says he thinks the Buddha was a case of cosmic consciousness, but do you think he was?"

"I do not."

"Why exactly?"

"I see illumination, but I don't see cosmic consciousness. As I understand it, Nirvana means winning release from rebirth through the extinction of desire. It means reaching a state of 'extinguishednesss,' which, as I understand it, is like having all your desires blown out like a candle. I don't think that's the same as identifying with the cosmos. Therefore, based on what Bucke has given to us, I don't see Gautama as a case of cosmic consciousness. I think Bucke was seeing what he wanted to see in Gautama. And I think he was seeing what he wanted to see in the next person, too."

"Who's the next person?"

"Jesus—Jesus of Nazareth."

Jesus of Nazareth

"You're telling me you don't think Jesus experienced cosmic consciousness?" I cried.

"He may have. I just don't see any convincing evidence that he did," Ben said calmly.

I was incredulous.

"But what about his forty days and forty nights in the desert, where he fasted and was tempted by the quote-unquote devil? Couldn't that be where he had a momentous spiritual experience?"

"Who knows, he may have had some kind of mystical experience. Bucke does allude to the accounts of Jesus' time in the wilderness after his baptism by John the Baptist. He also mentions Jesus' transfiguration on a mountaintop, where Peter, James, and John saw Jesus shine with bright rays of light, while Moses and Elijah appeared beside him. He hints that those accounts could be suggestive of Jesus having attained cosmic consciousness. But he thinks there are even more convincing reasons for thinking Jesus experienced it."

"Which are?"

"He thinks they can be found in the sayings and parables of Jesus."

Ben looked down at the book and turned a few pages.

"Here listen to this. It's the very first example Bucke gives. It's from Matthew chapter 5, verse 3: *Blessed are the poor in spirit for theirs is the kingdom of heaven.* For this passage, Bucke proposes that Jesus is actually saying: *A proud man is hardly likely to acquire the cosmic sense.* When Jesus says 'kingdom of heaven' Bucke assumes Jesus is referring to the cosmic sense, or cosmic consciousness. In other words, if you are poor in spirit—

meaning not proud—then you can acquire cosmic consciousness. But I think Bucke's interpretation rests on many unfounded assumptions."

"Such as?"

"To begin with, it assumes that Jesus was trying to guide his followers to cosmic consciousness in the same way that Gautama was trying to guide his followers to Nirvana. But how do we know that?"

"Because he says *heaven*. He wanted us all to get to heaven, to get to cosmic consciousness."

"To be precise, he says *kingdom of heaven*. But during Jesus' time, what was kingdom of heaven really referring to? Kingdom of heaven in the New Testament is used interchangeably with *kingdom of God*. In fact, kingdom of God is used more often than kingdom of heaven in the New Testament books. It is only Matthew who uses the phrase kingdom of heaven. Mark and Luke use the phrase kingdom of God in their versions of the parables that correspond to Matthew's parables. And even Matthew himself uses kingdom of God sometimes. In one instance, he even says kingdom of God right after saying kingdom of heaven."

"Where does he do that?"

Ben got up from the futon and stepped over to the shelf against the wall. He picked up a small, faux-leather-bound Bible and sat back down. Opening it, he began to flick through its crinkly pages with small print. I could see yellow highlights in it also.

"Here it is. This is Matthew Chapter 19, beginning at verse 23: *Then Jesus said to his disciples, 'I tell you the truth, it is hard for a rich man to enter the kingdom of heaven. Again I tell you, it is easier for a camel to go through the eye of a needle than for a rich man to enter the kingdom of God.'* So you see, Matthew doesn't distinguish between the two terms kingdom of heaven and kingdom of God. They are equivalent for him."

"Okay, so kingdom of God or kingdom of heaven. I don't see how that makes that much of a difference."

"Well, it does, because the kingdom of God at that time was a political-religious term, not a mystical-spiritual term like Nirvana. Proclaiming the coming of the kingdom of God meant reestablishing God's kingdom—King David's kingdom—on earth."

"How do you know that?"

"At Jesus' time, Palestine was occupied by the Romans. So if you were calling yourself the Messiah—as Jesus did—and calling for the kingdom of God, that meant you were calling for the *rule* of God to be reestablished in Palestine, and that meant you were also calling for the *rule* of Caesar to be cast out. And that was treason. That was sedition. And the punishment for a state crime like that was execution by crucifixion. So preaching about the kingdom of God—or the kingdom of heaven—was a revolutionary call to purify Israel, expel the Roman occupiers, and disempower the corrupt priests of the Jerusalem Temple and the Jewish aristocracy, who were collaborating with the Romans to exploit the people of Israel."

"So you're saying Jesus was a revolutionary."

"Yes, but not in the secular sense of today—not in the same way that you would think of George Washington, Robespierre, or Lenin. That's because religion and politics were intertwined during Jesus' time. So yes, keeping all that in mind, Jesus was a revolutionary. Definitely."

Ben flicked through the little Bible's crinkly pages.

Here, listen to what he said in his very first sermon when he returned to his native Nazareth. It's in Luke chapter four. *Jesus returned to Galilee in the power of the Spirit, and news about him spread through the whole countryside. He taught in their synagogues, and everyone praised him. He went to Nazareth, where he had been brought up, and on the Sabbath day he went into the synagogue, as was his custom. And he stood up to read. The scroll of the prophet Isaiah was handed to him. Unrolling it, he found the place where it is written: 'The Spirit of the Lord is on me, because he has anointed me to proclaim good news to the poor. He has sent me to proclaim freedom for the prisoners and recovery of sight for the blind, to release the oppressed, to proclaim the year of the Lord's favor.'* So you see, Jesus was proclaiming the year of the Lord's favor. The year of the Lord's favor was the Jubilee Year. The Jubilee Year harkens back to Isaiah and Leviticus in the Old Testament. It called for the cancellation of debts, freeing those who had to work as bondservants, and returning lands to the people who had lost them due to debt foreclosure. And you can bet your life the Pharisees and the rich didn't want to hear Jesus calling for the year of the Lord's favor. They didn't want him calling for the Jubilee Year when the poor regained their liberty. Oh yes, Jesus was a revolutionary."

"But most revolutionaries condone violence, or at least think it might be necessary in some way. I don't think Jesus ever did that, did he?"

Ben flicked through pages of the little Bible again.

"This is from Matthew chapter 10, verse 34: *Do not suppose that I have come to bring peace to earth. I did not come to bring peace, but a sword.*"

"Okay, but then how do you account for him saying, 'Love your enemies' and 'Turn the other cheek'? That's pacifism—a sign of a spiritual man, not a revolutionary one, isn't it?"

"It certainly can be. But remember, Jesus was a Jew preaching to Jews. When Jesus said 'Love your enemies' and 'Turn the other cheek,' he meant that to apply to his fellow Jews—not to non-Jews, and certainly not to the Roman oppressors."

"A Jew preaching to Jews? I always thought Jesus' message was for everyone, everywhere."

"Well, it certainly became that, but that's not how it began with Jesus himself."

"How can you say that? How do you know that?"

"If you look at Jesus as a historian would, keeping him in his time and place and letting those things define him, then it's pretty clear. But if you assume he was a celestial spirit—if you mentally remove him from all the cultural and religious influences he was born into and grew up with—well, then you might see him speaking through a megaphone, broadcasting down through the generations, directly to everyone in every field and on every street corner in the great wide world for all time to come. But if, as I say, you look at him through a historical lens, you can see him as speaking directly to Jewish audiences: specific people with specific concerns who lived in the first century. You can see Jesus as a Jew—as an ethno-nationalist—preaching to his fellow Jews about Judaism and their Roman oppressors."

"Jesus as a Jewish revolutionary? An ethno-nationalist? That's quite a radical way to look at him. Where exactly do you see that?"

Ben flicked through pages in the little Bible again. He wetted his thumb and index finger to rub two pages apart that had stuck together.

"This is from Matthew, chapter 15, but similar versions can also be found in Mark and Luke: *The Faith of the Canaanite Woman—Leaving that place, Jesus withdrew to the region of Tyre and Sidon. A Canaanite woman from that vicinity came to him, crying out, 'Lord, Son of David, have mercy on me! My daughter is suffering terribly from demon-possession.' Jesus did not answer a word. So his disciples came to him and urged him, 'Send her away, for she keeps crying out after us.' He answered, 'I was sent only to the lost sheep of Israel.' The woman came and knelt before him. 'Lord, help me!' she said. He replied, 'It is not right to take the children's bread and toss it to their dogs.' 'Yes, Lord,' she said, 'but even the dogs eat the crumbs that fall from their masters' table.' Then Jesus answered, 'Woman, you have great faith! Your request is granted.' And her daughter was healed from that very hour.* So you see, for Jesus the Jews were the children, and the non-Jews were the dogs. Words like that could only come from someone who strongly identified himself as a Jew, as an ethno-nationalist Jew."

Ben flipped a few pages back in the little Bible.

"In Matthew, in chapter 10, when he is sending out his twelve apostles to preach on their own, Jesus says to them: *Do not go among the Gentiles or enter any town of the Samaritans. Go rather to the lost sheep of Israel.* So, I think it's pretty clear who Jesus' message was for. It wasn't for everyone, everywhere. It wasn't even for nearby villages—unless they were Jewish."

Ben observed me as I thought about what he had said. After a few moments, I came up with a counterpoint.

"Okay, but what about Jesus' enlightened morality—even if it was only for the Jews? Wasn't that an indication of spiritual development? What about statements like 'Love your neighbor as yourself'? That was a big deal, wasn't it? Nobody before in the world had come up with a moral precept like that. Had they?"

"Actually, that was already in the Old Testament."

Ben fanned back the pages in the little Bible.

"This is from the Old Testament book of Leviticus, chapter 19 verse 18: *Do not seek revenge or bear a grudge against one of your people, but love your neighbor as yourself. I am the Lord.* Of course, neighbors here meant fellow Jews."

"So you're saying Jesus was basically a political figure—not a spiritual figure at all?

"It depends on how you define spiritual. In the case of Gautama, the narratives are pretty clear that he was concerned with his own personal spiritual development to begin with. Then, after he attained his own enlightenment, he became a teacher who was concerned with other people's spiritual development, how they could attain the same spiritual state that he had. In Jesus' case, the Gospels tell of a man who had illuminating experiences and miraculous healing powers. But Jesus didn't tell people how to gain those illuminating experiences or healing powers. Instead, he spoke in parables about the kingdom of God, which Jewish leaders found threatening and Roman occupiers viewed as seditious—so much so that they executed him."

"You left out his coming back from the dead."

"Yes, I did. If you wish to believe he came back from the dead, you are free to do so."

"So, all in all, are you saying that Bucke was wrong to suppose that Jesus was a case of cosmic consciousness?"

"What I'm saying is that Bucke's contention that the sayings and parables of Jesus prove he must have had a cosmic consciousness experience is wishful thinking. I think Bucke was simply seeing what he wanted to see in the New Testament sayings and parables of Jesus. If Jesus was trying to teach people about his enlightenment and cosmic consciousness experience, why would he choose to speak in parables that are often so hard to understand? Why make the message so convoluted? And actually, there's evidence that he was deliberately trying to make his message ambiguous."

"Where's that?"

Ben wetted his fingertips and turned several pages forward in the little Bible.

"This is from Mark, beginning at chapter 4, verse 10: *When he was alone, the Twelve and the others around him asked him about the parables. He told them, 'The secret of the kingdom of God has been given to you. But to those on the outside everything is said in parables so that they may be ever seeing but never perceiving, and ever hearing but never understanding...'* Doesn't it make more sense that Jesus was speaking in an obscure way—in a kind of secret code—because he was spreading a dangerous religious-political message, rather than an apolitical spiritual message? Jesus was saying the rich had to become poor and the poor, rich. If you went around saying that today with a very large crowd of people swarming around you, what do you think would happen? In Jesus' time, crucifixion was reserved for traitors, rebels, and bandits. The Romans would not have executed Jesus if he was just preaching about some pie in the sky thing. Jesus was a rebel. He considered himself the Messiah, the Anointed One, whose mission it was to recreate the kingdom of David, to usher in the rule of God. So it makes sense that he would want to conceal his message and make it a kind of secret code. Jesus was not a fool. At the very least, he was an extraordinary man. He was a hero and a zealot like the American anti-slavery zealot, John Brown. I can't fathom the courage it took for him to take on the powerful political forces of his day. So no, I'm not saying it was completely wrong for Bucke to suppose that Jesus was a case of cosmic consciousness. It's not unwarranted to suppose that Jesus might have had some kind of consciousness-altering experience in his life—most likely in the desert wilderness—that enabled him to become the person he became, and to lead a revolt against the corrupt Temple elite and the Roman Empire. But, all in all, since clear evidence is lacking—and certainly isn't found in the sayings and parables of Jesus—well, because of that, I think Bucke should have put him in his second category."

Ben put down the little Bible and picked up the *Cosmic Consciousness* book. He opened it to the table of contents.

"He should have put him in the part he calls: *Additional—Some of Them Lesser, Imperfect, and Doubtful Instances.*"

I stared at Ben, wondering what I had just been doing. Why had I been acting as Jesus' defense lawyer? What was I trying to prove? I had always thought of myself as an atheist—ever since that day in eighth grade when I proved to myself there was no God by striding past my school's church while uttering a curse word at the 'God' inside. He didn't strike me dead. Nor did I trip or stub my toe on the way home. For all those years since, thinking myself an atheist hadn't seemed to make much of a difference. I must still have thought Jesus was some kind of god. Some kind of otherworldly, divine being. I guess some things run deeper than you think.

I nodded, signaling to Ben that I had no more questions.

"Okay," Ben said. "Let's move on to Bucke's next case of cosmic consciousness. He's the man who took Jesus of Nazareth—an ethno-religious revolutionary who was executed by Rome—and turned him into Jesus the Christ, the god of the world's largest religion. That man was Paul."

Paul

"How does Bucke think Paul is a case of cosmic consciousness?"

"In the same way he thinks all the individuals in his book are cases of cosmic consciousness. He sees cosmic consciousness as a manifestation of a sudden evolutionary change taking place in the individual. That's why, instead of always referring to it as *cosmic consciousness*, he also refers to it as the *cosmic sense*. In other words, as if it were actually a new, physical sense—a new literal faculty or capacity on top of our existing form of consciousness. But to me, cosmic consciousness is a psychological phenomenon. It's something that happens in the mind of the individual. The individual's consciousness *does* change, but it's a psychological change—not a physical or evolutionary one. Sure, you can think of it as a new *sense* or a new *faculty*, but unless you're using those terms metaphorically, you risk reifying or concretizing a psychological experience by describing it that way. It's similar to how people might turn consciousness into a kind of thing when they conceive of it as an eternal soul or an immortal entity that lives on after death. Yes, when you have a mystical experience—like cosmic consciousness—I do think something happens that changes your consciousness, but that change is the result of a psychological or mental event, not the eruption of an evolutionary process or the switching on of a genetic code in your DNA."

"Okay, that makes sense, but what explicit evidence does Bucke give for believing Paul is a case of cosmic consciousness?"

"Bucke's main reasons are Paul's writings and the events reportedly experienced by him on the road to Damascus."

"Damascus. I know about that," I said proudly. "That's when a powerful spotlight from the sky struck Paul like a laser beam, caused him to fall off his horse, and he heard Jesus Christ speak to him from heaven above."

Ben chuckled.

"Right, but actually I don't think we know if he was on a horse. Certainly no horse was mentioned in the Bible. You're probably getting that from the painting by Caravaggio."

"I don't know where I'm getting it, actually."

"In any case, the Damascus episode is described three times in the New Testament book of *Acts*. Each version is more or less the same. But Paul didn't write *Acts*—it was written by Luke, the same person who wrote the *Gospel of Luke*. It's Luke who tells us about Paul's conversion, not Paul himself."

"That's odd."

"It is, isn't it? You'd think Paul would have described the Damascus incident in at least one of the thirteen New Testament epistles he's believed to have written. But perhaps Paul felt that Luke had done a good enough job telling the story, and so he didn't need to rehash it. Or perhaps he simply said he had a revelation from Jesus Christ and left it at that. Maybe Luke, being a talented public relations man, felt the need to create the Damascus story so Paul's followers would have something they could relate to emotionally. In any case, let's deal with the event as it's given to us."

Ben looked down at the book.

"Bucke includes the three versions of the Damascus incident found in the book of *Acts*. I'm going to read the second of the three. It's the one where Luke has Paul speaking in the first person. This version is from chapter 22: *And it came to pass, that as I made my journey, and drew nigh unto Damascus, about noon, suddenly there shone from heaven a great light round about me. And I fell to the ground and heard a voice saying unto me, Saul, Saul, why persecutest thou me? And I answered, Who art thou, Lord? And he said unto me, I am Jesus of Nazareth, whom thou persecutest: And they that were with me beheld indeed the light, but they heard not the voice of him that spake to me. And I said, What shall I do, Lord? And the Lord said unto me, Arise and go into Damascus. And there it shall be told thee of all things which are appointed for thee to do. And when I could not see for the glory of that light, being led by the hand of them that were with me, I came into Damascus.*"

Ben looked up at me.

"That's a pretty amazing experience, isn't it?" I said, raising my eyebrows.

"Yes, it's a powerful story," Ben replied thoughtfully. "Especially when you consider that before this experience Paul identified completely with Judean religious law—so much so that he even became a hardline enforcer of it. A letter-of-the-law kind of guy, he persecuted Christians wherever he could find them. That's actually why he was going to Damascus—to root out the Christians there, oppress them, and bring them to Jewish justice. But after this experience, he did a complete mental turnaround—one hundred and eighty degrees—from hating Jesus of Nazareth to identifying with him and becoming a true believer in Jesus as the risen Christ, the Messiah. From there, he went on to become the great evangelist of Jesus as the Christ, proclaiming him as a god to the Gentiles— the entire civilized world beyond the Jewish sphere. Of course, these days we can't take the Damascus episode literally. We can't believe that an external light—or, as you put it, a spotlight—from high up in the sky shone down on him while Christ, also high up in the sky, spoke to him. It seems to me that today we can understand it only as either an external projection of an internal psychological experience or as the sensational writing of a public relations man."

"Yes, of course. But if Luke didn't make it up, and it was, as you say, an external projection of an internal psychological experience, how does that happen?"

"What makes sense to me is the way Jungian psychologists might explain it. Paul's ego-consciousness was completely identified with Jewish law, but his unconscious felt differently. These two opposing psychic forces were at war with each other until, finally, a crisis occurred. Paul's unconscious burst forth as 'Christ' and spoke thunderously to him, demanding to know why he was persecuting him. This experience shattered Paul's rigid ego-consciousness, which had been identifying with abstract religious-legal concepts. It even caused a physical reaction: Paul lost his sight and had to be led by the hand into Damascus. After a few days, he integrated the experience into his newly opened and expanded ego-consciousness, and he became a Christian. For him, this was a higher form of consciousness."

"But how can that happen? How can a psychological event become externalized like that? How can the unconscious do that sort of thing?"

"How do you dream? How does the unconscious create lifelike movies in your mind when you sleep at night— movies that your waking consciousness has no control over? If you want, you can think of Paul's Damascus experience as a waking dream. Perhaps this would have normally been a nightmare, but it was so powerfully charged that it broke through into Paul's waking consciousness. Who knows, maybe, in reality, it was a dream. Perhaps the episode Luke wrote should have begun with: *In my dream, I was on my way to Damascus.* Maybe it happened in the dream world or in the waking world— or maybe it didn't happen at all the way Luke said it did. Either way, I think we can assume Paul had some sort of psychological experience that profoundly affected him."

"And that experience was reflected in Paul's writings?"

"Yes. And while Bucke interprets Paul's writings as evidence of an evolutionary change, I interpret them as evidence of a psychological event."

Ben looked back down at the book, turned the page, and scanned it.

"Here's an example. It's an excerpt Bucke includes from Paul's epistle to the Galatians from chapter 1, beginning at verse 11: *For I make known to you, brethren, as touching the gospel which was preached by me, that it is not after man. For neither did I receive it from man, nor was I taught it, but it came to me through revelation of Jesus Christ.* Here, Paul is simply saying that his gospel— his preaching—stems from a revelation of Jesus and not from any other source, such as the Old Testament or the disciples. However, Bucke claims that Paul's gospel came from the cosmic sense itself. Bucke writes, *As regards his 'Gospel,' Paul was instructed by the Cosmic Sense only. He knew, however, enough about Jesus and his teachings to be able to recognize (when it came to him) that the teachings of the Cosmic Sense were practically identical with the teaching of Jesus.* So, even though Paul himself claims that his gospel comes from a revelation of Jesus, Bucke believes Paul experienced cosmic consciousness and then simply equated it with Jesus' teachings, choosing to portray it as a revelation of Jesus."

"In a somewhat convoluted way, Bucke seems to be presuming a lot."

"Plainly. Of course, today, if someone said Jesus or God had spoken to them—or even if they told an elaborate Damascus-like story about how Jesus or God had spoken to them—we would naturally assume it happened within their own mind. And that's how we must think about Paul in his time: it was happening in his mind, his unconscious mind. And actually, Paul practically says so. Here's the next excerpt that Bucke cites. It's also from Galatians, chapter 1, beginning at verse 15: *But when it was the good pleasure of God, who separated me, even from my mother's womb, and called me through his grace to reveal His Son in me, that I might preach him among the gentiles...* Notice that Paul says, 'His Son *in me*.' So Paul feels that Jesus is inside him—not outside, up in the sky speaking to him, as in the Damascus story. Jesus is within Paul. The gospel—the preaching—originates from the Jesus Christ within him. It comes from Paul's psychological state, from his mind."

"Yes, I can see that now."

Ben turned the page in the book.

"Let me make one more comparison between Bucke's cosmic consciousness way of looking at Paul and my psychological way. Here's a famous excerpt from Paul's writings—you've probably heard it. It's from 1 Corinthians, chapter 13: *If I speak with the tongues of men and of angels, but have not love, I am become sounding brass, or a clanging cymbal.* And further on: *When I was a child, I spoke as a child, I felt as a child, I thought as a child; now that I am become a man, I have put away childish things. For now we see in a mirror, darkly; but then face to face: now I know in part; but then shall I know even as also I have been known. But now abideth faith, hope, love, these three; and the greatest of these is love.*"

Ben looked up at me.

"Obviously, this was a man who was full of hate and who had an experience that filled him with love—a wonderful thing. But even though Bucke saw love as the foundational principle of the world when he had his own cosmic consciousness experience, that doesn't mean Paul had to have a cosmic consciousness experience to realize that love is the greatest thing in the world."

"Why is that, exactly?"

"Because he could just as well have come to that realization through a psychological breakthrough—not because he experienced cosmic consciousness. If he had experienced cosmic consciousness, wouldn't he also have spoken of identifying with the cosmos and infinity—the primary indicators of the phenomenon? Instead, he identified with the Jesus Christ within him. Clearly, Paul's experience was a religious experience—a religious conversion. It was also a psychological turnaround. He was like Ebenezer Scrooge in Dickens' *A Christmas Carol*: a complete change of personality. He opened up. He turned around and had a complete change of heart. He went from being completely closed-minded to being completely open-minded. He went from being full of hate to being full of love. Don't get me wrong—I'm not saying that it wasn't a great spiritual transformation. I'm just saying I don't think it was a cosmic consciousness experience."

"Okay, let me get this straight. So far, you've covered three people: Buddha, Jesus, and Paul—and you don't think any of them was a definite case of cosmic consciousness. Is that right?"

"Yes, that's right. But let's move on, because I think you'll be relieved to know that I do believe the next person is a true case of cosmic consciousness."

"Okay, that's great. Who is it?"

"It's the Neoplatonic philosopher Plotinus."

Plotinus

Ben looked down at the book and turned a few pages.

"Here's an excerpt from a long letter he wrote to a friend of his named Flaccus: *You ask, how can we know the Infinite? I answer, not by reason. It is the office of reason to distinguish and define. The Infinite, therefore, cannot be ranked among its objects. You can only apprehend the Infinite, by a faculty superior to reason, by entering into a state in which you are your finite self no longer—in which the divine essence is communicated to you. This is ecstasy. It is the liberation of your mind from its finite consciousness. Like can only apprehend like; when you thus cease to be finite, you become one with the Infinite. In the reduction of your soul to its simplest self, its divine essence, you realize this union—this identity.*

But this sublime condition is not of permanent duration. It is only now and then that we can enjoy this elevation (mercifully made possible for us) above the limits of the body and the world. I myself have realized it but three times as yet, and Porphyry hitherto not once."

Ben looked up at me.

"What could be more straightforward than that? Do you remember what the subtitle of the book is?"

"Something about the infinite."

Ben held the book up so I could see the front cover.

"Oh right, that's it: *The Classic Investigation of the Development of Man's Mystic Relation to the Infinite.*"

"Yes, and Plotinus talks about the infinite. He speaks about apprehending it, identifying with it, becoming one with it—and experiencing ecstasy in the process. That's cosmic consciousness in a nutshell, isn't it?"

"Yes, I would think so. But I don't think I've ever heard of Plotinus. When did he live?"

"Let's see… I know he was born in Roman Egypt."

Using his thumb as a lever, Ben flipped back a page in the book.

"Here it is. Bucke says he was born in 204. So that means he was born about 200 years after Jesus and Paul. Bucke says he died in 274, so that means he was 70 years old when he died."

Ben turned a page and studied it. I could tell he was thinking, so I waited patiently, not wanting to interrupt him. Eventually, he looked up.

"Notice that this is the first of Bucke's instances of cosmic consciousness to mention the infinite. The infinite isn't mentioned by Buddha, Jesus, or Paul."

Ben looked toward the window, smiled thoughtfully, and said, "Plotinus's focus on the infinite makes me think of what I wrote on the chalkboard in my high school senior English class."

"What was that?"

"If I remember correctly, it was: *Born into a world of finitude, I realize my life is but an interruption to infinity.*"

"Why did you write that?"

"I don't know. It just occurred to me one day, and I came early to class and wrote it on the chalkboard."

"What happened when the teacher came in?"

"He read it and was puzzled by it. But he didn't dismiss it outright or criticize it. I could see him asking himself about it in his mind: *How can one interrupt infinity? It makes sense, but it doesn't. Could such a sentence even be logical?* He was stumped. I can't remember now if he asked who wrote it or if my classmates told him I did. He was a good guy though—Mr. Sauer. I remember he had us read *The Stranger* by Albert Camus. I think that was a little avant-garde for my high school at the time. He was a clever man, too. Unlike all the other teachers at the school, he had his desk in the rear of the classroom. That way, our backs were always to him, except when he came up to the lectern to lead a discussion or to scold us about our late or poorly written essays. Having his desk at the back of the classroom meant he never had to waste much time disciplining us. I don't think I ever had the nerve to look over my shoulder to see what he was doing back there after he had given us a writing or reading assignment. I don't think anyone else did either."

Ben's eyes drifted away for a few moments and then came back.

"Anyway," he announced, "let's move on, shall we?"

"Why not?" I replied. "Who's next?"

"Mohammed."

Mohammed

Ben bent his head toward the book.

"To provide evidence for Mohammed's cosmic consciousness experience, Bucke quotes an excerpt from the *Life of Mohammed* by Washington Irving."

"Washington Irving?" I exclaimed. "You mean the guy who wrote 'Rip Van Winkle?'"

"Yes," Ben chuckled. "That's the one."

"I love that story! He also wrote 'The Legend of Sleepy Hollow.'"

"Yes, he did. Anyway, here's what Washington Irving wrote: *As Mohammed, in the silent watches of the night, lay wrapped in his mantle, he heard a voice calling upon him. Uncovering his head, a flood of light broke upon him of such intolerable splendor that he swooned. On regaining his senses he beheld an angel in a human form, which, approaching from a distance, displayed a silken cloth covered with written characters. 'Read!' said the angel. 'I know not how to read!' replied Mohammed. 'Read!' repeated the angel, 'in the name of the Lord, who has created all things; who created man from a clot of blood. Read, in the name of the Most High, who taught man the use of the pen; who sheds on his soul the ray of knowledge and teaches him what before he knew not.' Upon this Mohammed instantly felt his understanding illumined with celestial light and read what was written on the cloth, which contained the decree of God, as afterwards promulgated in the Koran. When he had finished the perusal the heavenly messenger announced: 'Oh Mohammed, of a verity thou art the prophet of God! And I am his angel Gabriel!'"*

Ben looked up.

"I have to say, it's psychologically very telling that Mohammed had a vision of an angel appearing before him and asking him to read."

"Why's that?" I asked, baffled.

"The consensus is that Mohammed was illiterate. He's actually known as the 'illiterate prophet.' He couldn't read or write—he says so himself in his vision. So why would such a man have a waking dream, a vision, that involved him inexplicably being able to read? Isn't that psychological compensation?"

"Psychological compensation?"

"Yes. You're ashamed of not being able to read and write. You feel inferior about it, so your unconscious creates a vision in which you miraculously overcome your defect. You can't read what humans write, but you *can* read what God writes. That is a special gift indeed! If Mohammed could read and write, would his vision have been different? Would he even have had a vision?"

"That's a fair question."

"But in any case, Mohammed did have the vision, and from that he went on to create the second-largest religion of the world, which is quite astounding when you think about it."

"Is Islam really the second biggest religion in the world?"

"It is. And those are basically the two reasons Bucke gives for believing Mohammed had a cosmic consciousness experience: one, the fact that he had a vision of an otherworldly power—namely, the angel Gabriel glowing with light; and two, that he is responsible for the Quran, the foundational text of the world's second-largest religion."

"I'm getting the feeling that you think Mohammed should be in the second category of cosmic consciousness candidates."

"Yes, that's more or less what I think. Once again, I take Bucke's cosmic consciousness experience as the model— the example *par excellence*. Bucke, however, is often quick to believe that if a person exhibits secondary aspects of his own cosmic consciousness experience—such as suddenness, intellectual illumination, subjective light, or a sense of immortality—then that person also had a cosmic consciousness experience, even though they lack the primary cosmic consciousness aspect of his own experience. I don't mean to diminish Mohammed's religious experience or downplay what he achieved. He was obviously an extraordinary man. I'm just saying it doesn't look to me like he had an literal cosmic consciousness experience."

"Yes, I can see that now. All right, who's next?"

Ben glanced at the book.

"Dante."

Dante

"He wrote the Divine Comedy, right?"

"That's right, he did," Ben replied, nodding. "And that seems to be the main reason Bucke believes that Dante had the cosmic sense. He thinks the first two books of the *Divine Comedy*—the *Inferno* and the *Purgatorio*—deal with the world of self-consciousness, whereas the last book, the *Paradiso*, deals with the world of cosmic consciousness."

"I've never actually read the *Divine Comedy*."

"I read it many years ago," Ben said, reminiscing, "so it is definitely not fresh in my mind. But what I remember is that it's a big, magnificent book—an epic religious poem, dealing with the Christian universe and the Christian afterlife. Dante wrote the *Divine Comedy* in the early 1300s, and for human beings living in the Western world at that time, life was essentially a kind of proving ground— a testing ground. How you lived your life—whether you were good or bad—determined where you ended up in the world that really mattered: the next world. Would you end up in hell—the Inferno—or find yourself in the place where you could be purified of your sins—the Purgatorio? Hopefully, as long as you had been good and pure enough, you would find yourself welcomed into heaven—the Paradiso. In the *Divine Comedy*, Dante travels through each of these realms with the help of a guide. In the *Inferno* and the *Purgatorio*, Dante's guide is Virgil, the Roman poet who wrote the *Aeneid*. In the *Paradiso*, Beatrice is his guide."

"Who was Beatrice?"

"Beatrice was his muse—his inspiration. In real life, she was a girl he met when they were both just nine years old. He fell in love with her at that first meeting and remained in love with her for the rest of his life, even though they were both married to other people. She died when she was only twenty-five years old, but his love for her didn't die. It lasted for the rest of his life, and he even granted her immortality by placing her into his masterpiece, the *Divine Comedy*."

Ben looked down at the book, turned two pages, and stopped.

"Here's what Bucke says in the latter part of the *Purgatorio,* where Virgil departs because Beatrice will be taking over as Dante's guide: *Virgil withdraws. The self-conscious mind abdicates its sovereignty in presence of the greater authority. Dante comes into immediate relation with Beatrice—Cosmic Consciousness.* Bucke's idea that Virgil represents the self-conscious mind—and therefore has to be replaced by Beatrice as Dante's guide to cosmic consciousness—is definitely not the traditional interpretation."

"What is the traditional interpretation?"

"The traditional interpretation is that Virgil had to be replaced because he was a pagan and should therefore not be allowed to guide Dante into or through the Christian heaven of the *Paradiso*."

"So what do you think? Was Dante a case of cosmic consciousness?"

"Dante might have had a cosmic consciousness experience. I just don't know for sure, because he never really said so. He wrote the *Divine Comedy,* which is certainly a great poem about the Christian cosmos, and there were probably a lot of inspiring and exciting realizations going on in his mind as he contemplated and envisioned those cosmological concepts. But did he actually have an ecstatic cosmic consciousness experience like Bucke's? If he did, he didn't write about it or about how it affected him personally. Not that I know of, anyway. Not like Plotinus did."

"But maybe it's in the *Divine Comedy* itself. Maybe he has himself as a character in the *Divine Comedy* describe the experience?

"Bucke does include some excerpts from the *Divine Comedy* that suggest Dante may have had a cosmic consciousness experience."

Ben turned the page.

"Here's the opening from the *Paradiso* that Bucke quotes: *The glory of Him who moves everything penetrates through the universe and shines in one part more and in another less. In the heaven that receives most of its light I have been, and have seen things which he who descends from there above neither knows how nor is able to recount.* Concerning this excerpt, Bucke writes: *So Paul heard 'unspeakable words,' and Whitman when he 'tried to tell the best' of that which he had seen became dumb.* Bucke suggests that when Dante says he is unable to recount what happened when he ascended to the heaven of Paradise, similar remarks are reflected in the writings of the apostle Paul and the American poet Walt Whitman. But did Dante actually have a cosmic consciousness experience that left him speechless in his own life? Or was Dante simply including it in the *Divine Comedy* because he had learned from sources like Paul that, when meeting God, you should not be able to put it into words?"

"That's a good question."

"Here's another excerpt from the *Paradiso* that Bucke cites: *Beatrice was standing with her eyes wholly fixed on the eternal wheels, and on her I fixed my eyes from there above removed. Looking at her, I inwardly became such as Glaucus became on tasting of the herb which made him consort in the sea of the other gods. Transhumanizing cannot be signified in words; therefore, let the example suffice…*

"Read that part about Glaucus again, would you?"

Ben smiled and nodded. He looked back down at the book and read:

"*I inwardly became such as Glaucus became on tasting of the herb which made him consort in the sea of the other gods.*"

"Okay, I confess I've never heard of Glaucus. Who was he exactly?"

Ben glanced back down at the book.

"Let's see… yes, here it is. According to Bucke, Glaucus was the steersman of the ship *Argo* who was changed into a god."

"Oh, from *Jason and the Argonauts*."

"Yes, that's right."

"Fascinating! So Glaucus became a kind of fish-god. That's so interesting! I keep learning more things about Greek mythology."

"Yes, but the question is, did Dante have an actual ecstatic cosmic consciousness experience in his own life, which he decided to put into the *Divine Comedy* in the form of Glaucus' transhumanizing experience? Or was he just trying to imagine what someone's experience would be like at that point in the story and decided to let Glaucus' experience represent it? If Dante had had an ecstatic cosmic consciousness experience, wouldn't he have told someone about it? And as far as I know, Dante never wrote about having a mystical experience in any letters to his family or friends."

"So why do you think Plotinus wrote about his cosmic consciousness experience and Dante didn't?"

"I think it's probably because Dante didn't actually have one."

"So then, the question becomes, why did Plotinus have a cosmic consciousness experience while Dante didn't—right?"

"Yes, and I have a theory about that, if you would like to hear it."

"I sure would."

"I think it's because their worldviews were different."

Ben put the *Cosmic Consciousness* book on the coffee table. He stood up, walked across the room to pick up *The Decline of the West,* and returned to his seat. He opened it up to reference grids at the back of the book. Unfolding the first one, TABLE I. 'CONTEMPORARY' SPIRITUAL EPOCHS, he pointed to Plotinus near the top of the Arabian column, then to Dante, who was at the same level in the Western column.

"See, Plotinus and Dante are 'contemporaries.' They are both in the *Earliest Mystical-Metaphysical Shaping of the New World-Outlook* phase, but they are in different high-cultures. Plotinus is in the Arabian, and Dante is in the Western."

"But why is Plotinus in the Arabian culture column? I thought he was Roman. Why isn't he in the Classical column?"

"That's because Plotinus was born in Egypt, and even though Egypt was under Roman rule at the time Plotinus lived, he really had the world-feeling and outlook of the Arabian culture. Plotinus, in his metaphysical writings called the *Enneads,* described three fundamental principles: the One, the Intellect, and the Soul. Everything we experience emanates from the One. Our goal, as Plotinus saw it, was to merge with the One. Couldn't that be why he had a cosmic consciousness experience? In the West, we're encouraged to have a *relationship* with God; but, generally speaking, we're really not encouraged to *merge* with God, are we?"

"Not that I know of."

"Dante travels through the three levels of the Christian cosmos, but he mainly observes things. That's the case even when he gets to Paradise. He beholds God there, and he stands in awe of Him and His heaven, but he doesn't try to merge with Him."

"Okay, so as far as cosmic consciousness goes, Dante is a maybe, is that right?"

"Yes, it looks that way to me."

"Very well, who's next?"

Ben placed *The Decline of the West* on the coffee table and picked up the *Cosmic Consciousness* book. He opened it and found the page he was looking for.

"Bartolomé Las Casas"

Bartolomé Las Casas

"Never heard of him."

"I confess I hadn't either," Ben said, knitting his eyebrows. "According to Bucke, he was a Spanish aristocrat who went to the New World in 1502, settling on an estate in Hispaniola. He was a slaveholder but also a priest. When he was preparing his sermon one day, he came upon some verses in the Bible which made him realize slavery was evil. Bucke believes that this was a cosmic consciousness moment for Las Casas."

"What were the verses?"

Ben turned the page.

"They were from the thirty-fourth chapter of Ecclesiasticus:

The Most High is not pleased with the offerings of the wicked; neither is he pacified for sin by the multitude of sacrifices.

The bread of the needy is their life; he that defraudeth him thereof is a man of blood.

He that taketh away his neighbor's living slayeth him; and he that defraudeth the laborer of his hire is a shedder of blood."

"Do you think those verses produced a cosmic consciousness moment in Las Casas?"

"I can't say for sure. Still, I think those words at least led him to a realization about slavery—which, don't get me wrong, was a very momentous thing—but I don't know that it caused him to have a cosmic consciousness experience, where he felt the ecstatic presence of the cosmos itself. After all, I wasn't there, so I can't say for sure. But in my defense, none of Las Casas' writings that Bucke presents show that it was a cosmic consciousness event for him. Bucke assumes it is, though, based on Las Casas' advanced moral realizations relative to his historical time period."

"So he's in the maybe category of cosmic consciousness candidates?"

"Yes, the maybe category."

"Okay, who do we have next?"

Ben turned the page.

"John Yepes. He was also known as St. John of the Cross."

John Yepes (Called St. John of the Cross)
"Can't say I'm familiar with him."

"Neither can I," Ben said. "But in reading Bucke's section on Yepes, I learned that he was a Christian monk, priest, and mystic, who lived in the 1500s in Spain."

"So did he live at the same time as Las Casas?"

Ben thought for a moment, then turned back a few pages in the book.

"Let's see, Las Casas was born in 1474 and died in 1566."

Ben turned back to the Yepes section.

"Yepes was born in 1542 and died in 1591. So yes, their lives did overlap to some extent."

"That was the time of the Spanish Inquisition, wasn't it?"

"Yes, the Spanish Inquisition was established by Queen Isabella and King Ferdinand of Spain about sixty years before Yepes was born. By the way, did you know that the Spanish Inquisition lasted until the early 1800s?"

"Are you kidding me? It lasted that long?"

"I know. It's hard to believe," Ben said, narrowing his eyes. "The Spanish Inquisition's presumed purpose was to combat heresy in Spain, but it was actually about consolidating power in the monarchy of the newly unified Spanish kingdom. It certainly helps to know about the times a person lived in to better understand them. I mean, if it was in Yepes's nature to be a mystic, given his environment, could he really have been any other kind of mystic besides a Christian mystic? Anyway, Bucke thinks that even though Yepes was a Christian mystic, his mysticism bore the marks of cosmic consciousness. He even thinks he knows exactly when Yepes had his cosmic experience."

Ben looked down at the book.

"He says that: *For originating, or adhering to, some monastic forms he was, in 1578, imprisoned for some months, and it was during this time, at the age of thirty-six, that he entered Cosmic Consciousness.*"

Ben turned the page.

"Bucke goes on to say: *The phenomenon of the subjective light seems to have manifested itself with unusual intensity in this case. Others are said to have seen it. Also it is said to have lighted him about the monastery. These latter statements doubtless rest upon exaggeration or confusion such as is found in the description of the same phenomenon in Paul's case. It is curious, too, that in the case of John Yepes, partial blindness, lasting some days, followed, and was evidently in some way connected with the subjective light.* Bucke says it was after this episode that Yepes wrote several books. Here's an excerpt Bucke cites from Yepes's book *Ascent of Mount Carmel*: *It is clearly necessary for the soul, aiming at its own supernatural transformation, to be in darkness and far removed from all that relates to its natural condition, the sensual and rational parts. The supernatural is that which transcends nature, and, therefore, that which is natural remains below. Inasmuch as this union and transformation are not cognizable by sense or any human power, the soul must be completely and voluntarily empty of all that can enter into it, of every affection and inclination, so far as it concerns itself."*

"Supernatural transformation? What do you think of that?"

"Well, I think it can actually be thought of as directions on how to reach a mystical experience, although it's couched in terms that a Christian mystic in 16th century Spain would use. In the note next to the excerpt, Bucke basically says that Yepes was describing a kind of yoga meditation:

This is the doctrine of the suppression and effacement of thought, and the subjection of desire taught by the Hindu illuminati from the time of Buddha until today—a doctrine undoubtedly resting on actual experience."

"It's incredible that a Christian mystic in the 16th century was doing a kind of yoga, isn't it?"

Ben looked toward the window.

"Yes, that is something, isn't it?"

I followed Ben's eyes. I could tell he was thinking about something. Whatever it was, he didn't want to or wasn't ready to share it. He looked back down at the book.

"Bucke adds another note below this one, saying that he thinks the author of the *Bhagavad-Gita* is a case of cosmic consciousness. But he didn't include him in the book because he didn't know enough about his personal life. He also believes that Krishna in the *Bhagavad-Gita* represents the cosmic sense, and that Krishna's speeches are the utterances of cosmic consciousness."

"Note to self," I said with a chuckle, "read the *Bhagavad-Gita* one of these days."

"Yes, and I'm going to have to re-read it one of these days myself," Ben added. "Well, let's finish up with Yepes. This is what Bucke says before he presents another excerpt from Yepes's book *Ascent of Mount Carmel: One of the characteristics of the Cosmic Sense many times touched, and to be touched, upon is the identification of the person with the universe and everything in the universe.* And here's part of that excerpt which shows that Yepes identified with the universe: *The heavens are mine, the earth is mine, and the nations are mine! Mine are the just, and the sinners are mine; mine are the angels and the Mother of God; all things are mine, God himself is mine and for me, because Christ is mine and all for me.* But of course, being a Christian mystic, Yepes couldn't help but include all the theological aspects of Christianity that he was steeped in and schooled in from his formative years through adulthood. So when he identified with the universe, it was a Christian universe."

"So would you leave him in the cosmic consciousness category that Bucke puts him in?"

"Yes, I think this man must have had one or more ecstatic cosmic consciousness experiences. Based on what was written about Yepes and what he himself wrote, I think Bucke was right to consider him an instance of cosmic consciousness."

"All right. Who's next?"

"Francis Bacon."

Francis Bacon

"Francis Bacon! The very man Mark Twain thought was Shakespeare?"

"Yes, and Bucke also thought Bacon was Shakespeare—very adamantly, in fact."

"So Bucke thinks that Bacon was Shakespeare *and* that he had cosmic consciousness."

"Precisely."

"What do you think?"

"First of all, I have to say that I don't think Francis Bacon was Shakespeare."

"Oh right, you thought he was the 13th Earl of Oxford or something."

"The 17th Earl of Oxford, Edward De Vere. But let's not get into that again, or we'll never finish this book. Suffice it to say that Bucke contends Shakespeare—whoever he was, whether Bacon, De Vere, or the man from Stratford-upon-Avon named William Shakespeare—possessed cosmic consciousness. But I don't see any evidence that he did. That I know of, he never wrote about having an experience of cosmic consciousness."

"So what evidence does Bucke give, then?"

"According to Bucke, the proof that Shakespeare had cosmic consciousness can be found in Shakespeare's sonnets."

"I admit I've never read those."

"Shakespeare's sonnets are 154 love poems. The first 126 of them are written to a young man, while the remaining 28 are written to a lady. But Bucke ignores those last 28. Instead, he focuses on the first 126, claiming they are not actually addressed to a young man, but are really addressed to the cosmic sense itself."

"Why does Bucke think that?"

Ben looked down at the book and flipped forward—one, two, three pages.

"Here's what Bucke says: *It is not absolutely denied that the first one hundred and twenty six 'Sonnets' can be read as if addressed to a young male friend (although in the case of several this might be, it seems to the writer, successfully disputed), but it is clear that so read they lack meaning and dignity—that, in fact, looked at from this point of view, they are entirely unworthy of the man (whoever he was) who wrote 'Lear' and 'Macbeth.'*

Ben looked up from the book.

"They lack meaning and dignity? They are entirely unworthy of the man? What can we say about this attitude of Bucke's? He clearly had a problem with homosexuality. I don't know what else to say. We know Bucke had a cosmic consciousness experience, but I guess having that experience doesn't necessarily change a person's attitude about everything. It certainly didn't appear to change his attitude toward homosexuality."

"So you don't think the sonnets could be read the way Bucke reads them—as being addressed to cosmic consciousness?"

"No, I do not. Why shouldn't we read them the way Shakespeare wrote them? He wrote the first 126 of them to a young man. Why do we have to insert cosmic consciousness in place of the young man? Bucke presents 22 of Shakespeare's sonnets along with commentary on why they prove Shakespeare had cosmic consciousness. It's very exasperating. When it comes to his belief that Shakespeare possessed cosmic consciousness, Bucke turns into a cyclops. He had an eye for only one thing. Here, I'll

give you an example. This is Sonnet 18. It's famous—you
might have heard of it."

Ben flipped through a few pages in the book and began
to read:

"Shall I compare thee to a summer's day?
Thou art more lovely and more temperate:
Rough winds do shake the darling buds of May,
And summer's lease hath all too short a date:
Sometime too hot the eye of heaven shines,
And often in his gold complexion dimm'd;
And every fair from fair sometimes declines,
By chance, or nature's changing course, untrimm'd;
But thy eternal summer shall not fade,
Nor lose possession of that fair thou owest;
Nor shall Death brag thou wander'st in his shade,
When in eternal lines to time thou growest:
So long as men can breathe, or eyes can see,
So long lives this, and this gives life to thee."

"Oh yes, I know that sonnet. Well, the first few lines
anyway."

"Now this is what Bucke says about this sonnet: *The*
first part of the sonnet is a eulogy of the Cosmic Sense. It
would seem that at the time this sonnet was composed
Bacon had settled in his own mind how the Cosmic Sense
was to express itself, and some of the work seems to have
been done—that is, some of the plays written. He speaks of
the Cosmic Sense as having grown to time in eternal lines.
Listen to that. He takes a beautiful love poem and somehow
wrestles it into being a secret manifesto about cosmic
consciousness. Ridiculous!"

Ben stopped talking abruptly and smoothed his
eyebrows, spreading the tips of his left thumb and index

finger over them. Then he flicked several pages forward in the book.

"Here's how he sums up his case for all this: *The first one hundred and twenty-six sonnets seem to show beyond doubt that their author had the Cosmic Sense and that these sonnets were addressed to it. It does not seem to the present writer that they can be made sense of (intelligently read) from any other standpoint.*"

Ben dropped the book in his lap and looked up at me. Raising his hands and eyebrows at the same time, he let out a sigh of exasperation.

"So, put Shakespeare in the maybe category?" I asked cautiously.

"Yes. Based on Shakespeare's actual work, he deserves that honor, I guess."

"And so we move on to...?"

"Jacob Behmen," Ben said, picking up the *Cosmic Consciousness* book again.

Jacob Behmen

"Another one I confess I've never heard of."

"That's okay—hardly anyone today has. He was a German shoemaker who lived in the 17th century. In my opinion, this man experienced cosmic consciousness. All I have to do is read a few excerpts Bucke includes in his section on Behmen to prove it to you."

"Finally, an easy one."

Ben smiled and nodded, then tilted his head down toward the book.

"This first excerpt is not directly from Behmen, but from a biography about him: *"Sitting one day in his room his eyes fell upon a burnished pewter dish, which reflected the sunshine with such marvelous splendor that he fell into an inward ecstasy, and it seemed to him as if he could now look into the principles and deepest foundation of things. He believed it was only a fantasy, and in order to banish it from his mind he went out upon the green. But here he remarked that he gazed into the very heart of things, the very herbs and grass, and that actual nature harmonized with what he had inwardly seen."*

Ben turned one page, then another.

"Here's another one, and this one is taken directly from Behmen's writings: *If you will behold your own self and the outer world, and what is taking place therein, you will find that you, with regard to our external being, are that external world."*

"That's kind of amazing, isn't it?" I blurted out. "I mean, for him to say that a person and the world are one and the same—that was really something, wasn't it?"

"Yes, it certainly was. Behmen identified with the external world. Just think about that. Isn't that cosmic consciousness?"

"I would think so."

Ben turned the page.

"Now here's another one. Keep in mind that Behmen lived in 17th-century Germany, so he was a Christian, and his cosmic consciousness was mixed in with his faith: *For Jesus Christ, the Son of God, the Eternal Word in the Father (who is the glance, or brightness, and the power of the light eternity), must become man, and be born in you if you will know God; otherwise you are in the dark stable, and go about groping and feeling, and look always for Christ at the right hand of God, supposing that he is a great way off; you cast your mind aloft above the stars and seek*

God, as sophisters teach you, who represent God as one afar off, in heaven."

"That's an interesting take on God becoming man…" I said, thinking out loud. "Not so he can save you and forgive your sins, but so he can be born *in* you."

"It is, isn't it? Okay, finally, before we move on, let me read you one last quote and see if you can tell me who it reminds you of: *It is in thee, and if thou canst for awhile cease from all thy thinking and willing thou shalt hear unspeakable words of God."*

"That's yoga meditation again! Just like what's-his-name."

"Right. John Yepes—also known as Saint John of the Cross."

"Okay, well, our next candidate was someone who lived more than a hundred years after Jacob Behmen."

"Who was that?"

"William Blake."

William Blake

"Oh yes, he was a mystical poet. I read some of his poems in my survey of English literature class. He was a painter, too, wasn't he?"

"He was. He was a wonderful, visionary painter. He was also ahead of his time in many ways."

"In what ways?"

"He was against slavery, he was anti-authoritarian, and he believed in free love. He was definitely a radical democrat, and even leaned toward anarchism. But that was on the practical side of things. On the metaphysical side, his writings reflected a cosmic consciousness outlook."

Ben looked down at the book and turned a few pages.

"Here's an excerpt from Blake's writings that Bucke includes: *The world of imagination is the world of eternity. It is the divine bosom into which we shall all go after the death of the vegetated body. This world of imagination is infinite and eternal, whereas the world of generation, of vegetation, is finite and temporal. There exist in that eternal world the permanent realities of everything which we see reflected in this vegetable glass of nature.*"

"Yes, I can see the cosmic consciousness there when he refers to the infinite and the eternal."

"Yes, but it's pretty clear that Blake's outlook is basically Platonic."

"It is?"

"It sure is, especially when he says: *There exist in that eternal world the permanent realities of everything which we see reflected in this vegetable glass of nature.* That's just like Plato's eternal Forms, which are reflected in the objects of this world. Blake refers to Plato's world of Forms as the 'world of imagination.' Even though Blake uses different words, he's still describing Plato's dualistic universe. Plato's eternal, transcendent dimension of Forms becomes Blake's 'world of imagination.' And this world—this life you and I exist in right now—he calls the 'vegetable glass of nature.' The eternal world of the imagination shines, like light through glass, into this natural, time-based world we are in."

"Oh yes, I can see that now."

"But I have to say that even after considering writings like this—which definitely have a cosmic consciousness perspective about them—I can't agree with Bucke that Blake was an instance of cosmic consciousness."

"Really? Why not?"

"For the simple reason that—for all Blake's talent, and his was a prodigious, amazing talent, don't get me wrong—there is no evidence he ever wrote about having had a cosmic consciousness experience. None, at least, that Bucke includes."

"But how can you say that? You just quoted me something from Blake where he speaks about the infinite and the eternal. Aren't those the marks of cosmic consciousness?"

"Yes, they are. But when I wrote about infinity on the blackboard in my high school English class, had I experienced cosmic consciousness? No, I had not. If I had, I wouldn't be here right now trying to find a way to do so, would I? Talking or writing about infinity or eternity doesn't necessarily mean you've experienced those things."

"I guess not," I said, dropping my head slightly.

"Even Bucke admits there is no real evidence that Blake experienced cosmic consciousness. Listen to this—here's how he summarizes his section on Blake: *Specific details of proof are in this case, as they must inevitably often be, largely wanting, but a study of Blake's life, writings (he is not in a position nor is he competent to judge Blake from his drawings) and death convinces the writer that he was a genuine and even probably a great case.* So, even though Bucke admits there isn't really any proof, he still includes Blake in the section of his book that he reserved for instances of cosmic consciousness. Once again, I think Bucke sees what he wants to see—even when he himself admits the evidence isn't there!"

"But why does he say Blake's death partly convinced him? How did Blake die?"

Ben blinked slowly, as if trying to recall something, then turned back two pages in the book.

"Here's what Bucke says about Blake's death: *His illness was not violent, but a gradual and gentle failure of physical powers which nowise affected the mind. The speedy end was not foreseen by his friends. It came on a Sunday, August 12, 1827, nearly three months before completion of his seventieth year. 'On the day of his death,' writes Smith, who had his account from the widow, 'he composed and uttered songs to his Maker so sweetly to the ear of his Catharine that when she stood to hear him he, looking upon her most affectionately, said: 'My beloved, they are not mine—no, they are not mine!' He told her they would not be parted; he should always be about her to take care of her. To the pious songs followed, about six in the summer evening, a calm and painless withdrawal of breath; the exact moment almost unperceived by his wife, who sat by his side. A humble female neighbor, her only other companion, said afterwards: 'I have been at the death, not of a man, but of a blessed angel.'*"

"Sounds like he was a sweet man."

"Yes, it looks like he had a peaceful death," Ben added.

"So I can understand why you don't want to put him in the proven cases category, especially since he never wrote about having had the experience. But do you at least think he belongs in the maybe category?"

"Oh yes, he's definitely a maybe. Just like our next candidate."

"Who's that?"

"Balzac."

Honoré de Balzac

"Balzac? The French writer?"

"That's the one. And he wasn't just a French writer—he was a prodigious one. He wrote over 90 novels."

"My God! That's a lot. I haven't actually read anything by him. Isn't he known for writing risqué novels?"

"Yes, and that's probably because, as a realist, he had a passionate commitment to the real. And sex is part of reality, is it not? So why not write about it?"

"Of course. So why do you think Bucke argues Balzac is an actual case of cosmic consciousness, but you believe he should only be put in the maybe category?"

"Well, just like with William Blake, Bucke spends a lot of time giving us biographical information about Balzac. But he doesn't provide any real evidence that Balzac actually had an experience of cosmic consciousness. Bucke does include excerpts from Balzac's writings, but they don't describe anything of the kind."

Ben turned several pages in the book, scanning each one before stopping.

"Here's an excerpt Bucke cites from Balzac's philosophical novel *Louis Lambert: The world of ideas divides itself into three spheres—that of instinct; that of abstraction; that of specialism.* And here's what Bucke says about it: *There are in the intellect three stages— simple consciousness, self-consciousness, and Cosmic Consciousness.* So Bucke thinks Balzac's three spheres— instinct, abstraction, and specialism—correspond to simple consciousness, self-consciousness, and cosmic consciousness. Who knows, maybe Balzac did have an experience of cosmic consciousness at some point in his life, but Bucke doesn't really provide convincing evidence that he did. So just like William Blake, I think Balzac belongs in the maybe category."

"Very well, who's next?"

"Walt Whitman."

Walt Whitman

"All right! Cosmic consciousness comes to America!"

"You could say that," Ben laughed. "It turns out Bucke actually knew Walt Whitman and even wrote a biography of him."

"Really? Now that's interesting!"

"Here, listen to this: *The following brief description is taken from the writer's 'Life of Whitman,' written in the summer of 1880, while he was visiting the author.*"

"You're telling me Bucke wrote a book about Walt Whitman and actually spoke face to face with him—just like you and I are sitting here speaking face to face?"

"Yes."

"Does the brief description include Whitman's cosmic consciousness experience?"

"No, it does not. It's just basic information about Whitman—his physical appearance, personality, and the things he liked to do. Here, I'll read you some of the highlights."

Ben flipped the page.

"*He is six feet... moderately bald... on the side and back the hair is long, very fine and nearly snow white... the sides and lower part of the face are covered with a fine white beard... the ear is very large... I believe the poet's senses are exceptionally acute, his hearing especially... I have heard him speak of hearing the grass grow...*"

Ben flipped another page.

"Walt Whitman's dress was always extremely plain... he had no necktie at any time... Everything he wore and everything about him was always scrupulously clean... Walt Whitman, in my talks with him at that time, always disclaimed any lofty intention in himself or his poems..."

Ben flipped another page.

"His favorite occupation seemed to be strolling or sauntering about outdoors by himself, looking at the grass, the trees, the flowers, the vistas of light, the varying aspects of the sky, and listening to the birds, the crickets the tree frogs, the wind in the trees, and all the hundreds of natural sounds."

"If Bucke thinks Walt Whitman had cosmic consciousness, the details of his experience should be in his biography of him, shouldn't they?"

"You would think so. But I can't say for sure because I haven't read Bucke's biography of Whitman, and I don't know where I can find it."

"But surely he would have included the proof in the *Cosmic Consciousness* book itself, right?"

"You would think so—but he doesn't."

"Well, that's disappointing. Bucke had a cosmic consciousness experience, and you're telling me that Bucke didn't even ask Whitman if he had one or what his experience was like?"

"Apparently not."

"Then why does Bucke include Whitman in his list of cosmic consciousness instances?"

"As with the others, he thinks he sees evidence of cosmic consciousness in Whitman's biography and writings."

"Did you see any cosmic consciousness in his writings?"

"I saw hints of it in some of the writings that Bucke included. Here, I'll read you a few."

 "As in a swoon, one instant,
Another sun, ineffable full-dazzles me,
And all the orbs I knew, and brighter, unknown orbs;
One instant of the future land, Heaven's land.

...

Hast never come to thee an hour,
A sudden gleam divine, precipitating, bursting all these bubbles, fashions, wealth?
These eager business aims—books, politics, arts, amours,
To utter nothingness?"

Ben looked up at me.

"Some of those lines could be referring to a cosmic consciousness experience, I guess. Or they could just be inspired poetry. What do you think?"

"I wouldn't call them clear evidence of a cosmic consciousness experience. I still don't understand why Bucke didn't just ask Whitman if he'd had one and write about that."

"Neither can I," Ben said, frowning as he looked at the page. "That's why I'm putting Whitman in the maybe category."

"Yes, you should, I agree. It only makes sense. Who's next?"

"Edward Carpenter. He's actually the last one that Bucke thinks is an actual instance of cosmic consciousness."

Edward Carpenter

"Edward Carpenter? That's another one I've never heard of."

"Neither had I," Ben admitted, "but I think Bucke might be right about this one."

Ben turned the page.

"Here's what Bucke writes about Carpenter: *It was early in 1881, as he tells us, when in his thirty-seventh year, that Carpenter entered into Cosmic Consciousness. The evidence of the fact is perfectly clear, but it is not within the power of the writer to give details of illumination beyond those given below. As a direct result of the oncoming of the cosmic sense he practically resigned his social rank and became a laborer; that is to say he procured a few acres of land not many miles from Dronfield in Derbyshire, built upon it a small house and lived there with the family of a working man as one of themselves…. He retains his piano, and after his hours of manual toil will refresh himself with a sonata of Beethoven, for he is an accomplished musician. It is needless to say that he is a pronounced and advanced socialist—perhaps an anarchist. He is one with the people, the 'common' people (made so numerous, so common, said Lincoln, because God loves them and likes to see many of them.)…*"

Ben turned another page.

"*In a letter to the present writer, who had asked for certain facts about the new sense, he says: 'I really do not feel that I can tell you anything without falsifying and obscuring the matter. I have done my best to write it out in 'Towards Democracy'. I have no experience of physical light in this relation. The perception seems to be one in which all the senses unite into one sense. In which you become the object. This is unintelligible, mentally speaking. I do not think the matter can be defined as yet; but I do not know that there is any harm in writing about it.'"*

"Okay, it's pretty clear there that Carpenter is saying he experienced some sort of mystical state, at least," I said.

Ben nodded and flipped a few pages.

"Here's a passage from Carpenter's book *Towards Democracy*:

Lo! What mortal eye hath not seen nor ear heard—
All sorrow finished— the deep, deep
ocean of joy opening within—the surface sparkling.
The myriad-formed disclosed, each one and all, all things that are transfigured—
Being filled with joy, hardly touching the ground reaching cross-shaped with outstretched arms to the stars, along of the mountains and the forests, habitation of innumeral creatures, singing, joy unending—
As the sun on a dull morning breaking through the clouds—so from behind the sun another sun, from within the body another body—these shattered falling—
Lo! now at last or yet awhile in due time to behold that which ye have so long sought—
O eyes, no wonder you are intent."

Ben looked up from the book.

"I'm hearing a lot of cosmic consciousness in that, aren't you? Let me read a line from that again: *Being filled with joy, hardly touching the ground reaching cross-shaped with outstretched arms to the stars.* That certainly seems to be expressing the experience of ecstatic cosmic consciousness, which Carpenter told Bucke he saw no harm in writing about."

"I can see some of Bucke's own experience there—only in poetry, right?"

"Yes, I think so," Ben said. "Okay, that concludes the section of the *Cosmic Consciousness* book that Bucke titled *Instances of Cosmic Consciousness*."

I scratched my head.

"Remind me, how many did you think were actual instances of cosmic consciousness and how many were just maybes?"

Ben turned back to the front of the book and studied the table of contents.

"Let's see, of the fourteen that Bucke started with, I only agreed with four: Plotinus, John Yepes, Jacob Behmen, and Edward Carpenter. That's because they either spoke directly about having an experience like Bucke's or their writings clearly suggested such an experience. For me, the maybes were those who didn't really present evidence of having had an experience like Bucke's, nor did their writings strongly suggest it. So the maybes were Gautama the Buddha, Jesus the Christ, Paul, Mohammed, Dante, Bartolomé Las Casas, Francis Bacon, William Blake, Honoré de Balzac, and Walt Whitman."

"You know," I said hesitantly, "I can't help but think if Bucke was alive today, he would disagree with some of your maybes."

"He probably would," Ben said, rubbing his forehead. "I wish he were alive today. I'd like to talk to him about his cosmic consciousness experience and how he came up with his criteria for determining who actually attained it. I'd especially like to talk to him about why one of his maybes in particular shouldn't be a maybe."

"So you think that one of his maybes shouldn't even be a possible case of cosmic consciousness?"

"No, no. On the contrary, I think that person in particular should be a *prime* instance of cosmic consciousness."

"Why's that?"

"Because that person's experience of cosmic consciousness was more like Bucke's experience than anyone else's in the book. But before we get into that, let me summarize the other 34 individuals that Bucke placed in the *Lesser, Imperfect, and Doubtful Instances* section—the ones I'm calling maybes."

Ben turned back to the front of the book and found the *Lesser, Imperfect, and Doubtful Instances* section in the table of contents.

"I won't go into each individual in depth, but I'll briefly describe the ones who deserve special mention and group the remaining individuals according to their defining characteristics."

"That sounds like a good plan."

"Bucke begins this section of the book explaining that just as the cosmic sense can be thought of as the rising of the sun in a person's life, there are also instances where the sun of cosmic consciousness appears on the horizon, but does not rise to the full resplendence of its midday glory and brilliance. To be clear, these are the examples that I've been calling maybes, but Bucke calls them lesser, imperfect, and doubtful ones. In these cases, he looks for any of the marks of cosmic consciousness that he identified in the beginning of the book, marks such as subjective light, moral elevation, intellectual illumination, a sense of immortality, the loss of the fear of death, the loss of the sense of sin, and the transfiguration of the subject as witnessed by others.

Moses is the first person he cites. He considers him a probable case partly because the burning bush incident could be interpreted as an experience of the subjective light. Additionally, the shining of Moses' face when he descended from Sinai can be seen as an instance of transfiguration.

Gideon, the military leader from the Book of Judges, is considered a possible case of cosmic consciousness because the angel of Yahweh appearing to him can be seen as an instance of intellectual illumination.

Likewise, he thinks the prophet **Isaiah's** elaborate vision of the Lord sitting upon a throne suggests illumination and the oncoming of cosmic consciousness.

Socrates is considered a candidate for cosmic consciousness due to his commendable physical, moral, and intellectual qualities, as well as a particular incident in which he supposedly stood motionless from one morning to the next, trying to resolve a philosophical problem.

Laozi, the author of the *Tao Te Ching*, is included on the list primarily because he wrote that spiritually illuminated text.

The Indian saint **Ramakrishna Paramahansa** makes the list because he was an ecstatic mystic who practiced multiple world religions and is known for his many spiritually illuminating sayings.

Finally, to conclude this group of individual cases, there's a spiritualist who goes by the initials **J.B.B**. He's included on the list because he reportedly had an out-of-body experience in which his spirit left his body for twenty minutes looking down at it, hovering above it, and eventually returning to it."

"They had out-of-body experiences that long ago?"

"Evidently."

"Well, that's very interesting."

"Okay, I think most of the remaining individuals in this section can be categorized into one of two categories: the religious revelation and conversion category or the poetic-philosophical category. In the **religious revelation and conversion** category, I include individuals such as the French mathematician and philosopher **Blaise Pascal**, the Swedish theologian **Emanuel Swedenborg**, as well as a British army officer named James Gardiner and an American preacher named Charles G. Finney. There are also a number of individuals in this category who only gave their initials."

"Pascal is known for saying it's better to live your life assuming God exists than to live it assuming He doesn't—only to die and find out He does, right?"

"Something like that," Ben said, smiling. "Now, in the **poetic-philosophical** category, there are also several individuals who only provided their initials—just like in the religious revelation and conversion group. Then there are a few people who did provide their names, but I've never heard of them before, such as J. William Lloyd, Horace Traubel, and Paul Tyner. Lastly, there are famous individuals such as the philosopher **Benedict Spinoza**, along with poets and writers like **William Wordsworth, Alexander Pushkin, Ralph Waldo Emerson, Henry David Thoreau,** and **Alfred Tennyson.**"

Ben looked up at me.

"And speaking of Alfred Tennyson, did you know that he practiced a kind of yoga meditation?"

"Tennyson was a yogi? That's hard to believe!"

"I know. It surprised me too. Here, let me find that section."

Ben looked down at the book, and after some back and forth, he found the page on Tennyson.

"Here we are. Listen to this: *A kind of walking trance I have frequently had, quite up from boyhood, when I have been all alone. This has often come upon me through repeating my own name to myself silently till, all at once, as it were, out of the intensity of consciousness of individuality, the individuality itself seemed to dissolve and fade away into boundless being; and this not a confused state, but the clearest of the clearest, the surest of the surest, the weirdest of the weirdest, utterly beyond words, where death was an almost laughable impossibility, the loss of personality but the only true life.*"

"That's Tennyson speaking? That's astonishing—I always thought he was just a stuffy Victorian poet."

"I know. I know." Ben looked embarrassed. "I assumed he was too. I never read much Tennyson. It's amazing to learn that he used the technique of repeating his own name like a mantra to achieve a spiritual experience like that."

"Absolutely! It makes me want to read his poetry."

"Well, now it's time to talk about that individual who shouldn't, in my opinion, be in this *Lesser, Imperfect, and Doubtful Instances* section. You know, like Bucke, I think it's possible that many of the individuals in this book could have had a cosmic consciousness experience. But you have to wonder—if they did, why didn't they feel the need to write about it?"

"Yes, exactly."

"Well, one person in this section *did* feel the need to write about it."

"Who was it? What's his name?"

Ben smiled. He consulted the table of contents, then turned to a page near the end of the book.

"Unfortunately, we don't know *her* name. We only have her initials—**C.M.C.** She was born in 1844, and in my opinion, hers is the prime instance of cosmic consciousness. All I have to do to prove that is read passages from what she has written. So here goes: *So it went on and though to all appearance I was happy and full of life like other girls, there was always that undercurrent—a vein of sadness deep down, out of sight. Often as I have walked out under the stars, looking up into those silent depths with unspeakable longing for some answer to the wordless questions within me, I have dropped upon the ground in a perfect agony of aspiration. ...Passing over the interval between this time and September, 1893, as unimportant, except for the constant struggle within me, I proceed to describe, as well as may be, the supreme event of my life, which undoubtedly is related to all else, and is the outcome of those years of passionate search. ...What it was I knew not except that it was a great yearning—for freedom, for larger life—for deeper love. ...So I said: There must be a reason for it, a purpose in it, even if I cannot grasp it. The Power in whose hands I am may do with me as it will! ...At last, subdued, with a curious, growing strength in my weakness, I let go of myself! In a short time, to my surprise, I began to feel a sense of physical comfort, of rest, as if some strain or tension was removed. Never before had I experienced such* *a feeling of perfect health. I wondered at it. And how bright and beautiful the day! I looked out at the sky, the hills and the river, amazed that I had never before realized how divinely beautiful the world was! ...I felt myself going, losing myself. Then I was terrified, but with a sweet terror. I was losing my consciousness, my identity, but was powerless to hold myself. Now came a period of rapture, so intense that the universe stood still, as if amazed at the unutterable majesty of the spectacle! Only one in all the infinite universe! The All-loving, the Perfect One! The Perfect Wisdom, truth, love and purity! And with the rapture came the insight. In that same wonderful moment of what might be called supernal bliss, came illumination. I saw with intense inward vision the atoms or molecules, of which seemingly the universe is composed—I know not whether material or spiritual—rearranging themselves, as the cosmos (in its continuous, everlasting life) passes from order to order. What joy when I saw there was no break in the chain— not a link left out—everything in its place and time. Worlds, systems all blended in one harmonious whole. ...One day, for a moment, my eyes were opened. It was in the morning, in the early summer of 1894, I went out in a happy, tranquil mood, to look at the flowers, putting my face down into the sweet peas, enjoying their fragrance, observing how vivid and distinct were their form and color. The pleasure I felt deepened into rapture; I was thrilled through and through, and was just beginning to wonder at it, when deep within me a veil, or curtain, suddenly parted, and I became aware that the flowers were alive and conscious! They were in commotion! And I knew they were emitting electric sparks! What a revelation it was! The feeling that came to me with the vision is indescribable—I turned and went into the house, filled with unspeakable awe. ...There was and is still, though not so noticeable as earlier, a very decided and peculiar feeling across the brow above the eyes, as of tension gone, a feeling of more room. That is the physical sensation. The mental is a sense of majesty, of serenity, which is more noticeable when out of doors. Another very decided and peculiar effect followed the phenomena above described— that of being centered, or of being a center. ...The consciousness of completeness and permanence in myself is one with that of the completeness and permanence of nature. ...My feeling is as if I were as distinct and separate from all other beings and things as is the moon in space and at the same time indissolubly one with all nature."*

Ben looked up at me.

"Well, that's just amazing," I said, almost whispering. "Really stunning."

"I know," Ben agreed. "Now, that's what I call a cosmic consciousness experience."

"Truly! And we only know her as C.M.C.?"

"Unfortunately, that's right."

"What does Bucke say about her? Did he think she was a case of cosmic consciousness? Did he say why he put her in the maybe section of his book?"

"He never explained why he put her there, but he did make comments throughout her narrative on things she said and how they related to others he considered examples of cosmic consciousness."

"Who exactly?"

Ben looked back down at the book and flipped through pages as he read out the references.

"Carpenter, Balzac, Whitman, Mohammed, Dante, Behmen, and Yepes—who was also known as Saint John of the Cross."

"So why did he put her in the maybe section? It doesn't make sense."

"No sense at all."

"Too bad we only know her initials."

"Yes. That's a shame. But at least we have her story."

"Yes, that's the important thing."

Ben put the book down on the coffee table in front of us.

"Can I?" I asked, reaching for it.

"Feel free," Ben said, standing up. "How about some tea before you go?"

"Yes, please!"

I brought the *Cosmic Consciousness* book over to the table by the window and sat down. I opened it and began to browse through it. Now I could see the many times Ben had inserted yellow highlights and penciled notes. As I turned the pages, I recognized all the individuals he had mentioned, and I could see the highlighted excerpts he had read aloud. The book's font was normal-sized, but it became very small in the many places where Bucke included the excerpts from the writings of cosmic consciousness candidates or where he added his own comments. I now understood why Ben took so long to read this book: it was 384 pages of dense, thought-provoking material. But with the extensive small print, it was really double that—more like 800 pages. I sat there, perusing it and enjoying the passages that matched what Ben had read aloud.

When Ben came to the table with the tea, he performed his funny ritual again—pouring the tea into my cup from high up, smirking the whole time.

"What do you think her name was?" I asked after we had sipped some tea. "You know, what do you think her initials stood for?"

Ben looked at me with a puzzled expression at first, which slowly transformed into a bemused half-smile.

"You mean C.M.C.? Well, we can only guess."

"So how about Charlotte?" I offered.

"Charlotte?" Ben shrugged. "Why not? Yes, I like that."

"Also, I have to say her writing seems so modern, don't you think? It's very clear and simple. Not stilted or needlessly formal."

"Yes, it does seem like it was written by someone today, doesn't it? But she actually wrote it nearly a hundred years ago."

"I bet she smiled in photos too."

"In photos?"

"Yes, you know how people in photos from that time period always looked so serious. I bet you she smiled in photos."

Ben tilted his head slightly and looked upward, trying to imagine it.

"Yes, why not? Someone who experienced cosmic consciousness… in a group photo from that time period… everyone would be looking so stern and serious, but she would be smiling. She would stand out. Yes, I can see that."

We both took a sip of tea. We sat for a while, each thinking our own thoughts.

"You know," I said, breaking the silence, "now that I think about it—although it's wonderful what happened to C.M.C., I mean, our Charlotte—I can't help but wonder if she would have had her beautiful cosmic consciousness experience if the weather had been bad. You know, if a cold wind had been blowing or it had been raining that day?"

Ben seemed a little perplexed. He was thinking.

"You're right!" he suddenly exclaimed. "Who knows how much our spiritual lives depend on the weather? Who can say? But cold weather or warm weather, I intend to have a big realization like that—I mean a cosmic consciousness experience like that. I'm going to do it— especially now that I know that it's real and that others have experienced it."

"But how are you going to do it?"

"I don't know exactly—but I will."

He said this, looking at me with such a manic intensity that I was convinced if anyone could do it, he could. He would find a way.

When I was lying in bed that night, I began to think about my afternoon with Ben. I felt as if I had been through another semester-long, graduate-level course in a couple of hours. No—it was more like a *year*-long, graduate-level course. Undoubtedly, that was why I felt off-balance as I climbed the stairs to my apartment—just like the first time I left his place, after he had summarized the books on his table. But this session was even more intense and far-ranging than that. A person simply couldn't be expected to absorb that much mind-altering information in such a short span of time and still walk away as sure-footed as a gymnast.

Instead of trying to remember everything he'd talked about from beginning to end, I decided to let go, allowing my thoughts to float around in my mind and settle into my gray matter naturally.

Jesus came first. He would no longer be that luminous mystery in the back of my mind—not that otherworldly, grand religious figure and historical event that hovered around the outskirts of my everyday reality. Now, once and for all, he was truly a flesh-and-blood man with flashing eyes—like those of John Brown in the daguerreotypes I had seen in history books. That he was that, and only that, was as clear and certain as the bed I was lying on. As certain as the fact that Monday would come, and I would have to get up, drag myself down to Computer Connection, and suffer through another unending day of sales-floor drudgery.

What else could Jesus be, when you considered the times he lived in? The historian's Jesus. He was either that, or the luminous mystery I had allowed him to become even after I had proven to myself he wasn't God when I was in eighth grade. So why had I still let that glowing, mysterious version hang around like a cobweb in the back of my mind? Time to clean house completely.

Jesus was a man—an ethno-religious revolutionary who took on the awful powers of his time, the brutal Roman occupiers and their corrupt, Jewish, oligarchical collaborators—all in the name of the less fortunate, the poor, the abused—the people! And he had paid a horrible price for it. He was a hero, not a god, and his disciples were his comrades.

How many books must Ben have read to come to that point of view about Jesus? Obviously at least the Bible. That was plain to see when he pulled out his little Bible and readily produced the verses that supported his argument.

And Paul. He wasn't part of God's grand plan either. He was a Roman Jew with a divided self that became unified again when his unconscious identified with Jesus Christ. He was so grateful that the "Christ" in him had healed the rift between his conscious and unconscious selves that he decided to proclaim his own personal psycho-emotional drama as the solution to everyone's problems in the entire Roman world. He was like an alcoholic who overcomes his own addiction and decides that *this* is everyone else's problem, too—and that everyone in the world should give up alcohol.

Couldn't he just have quietly converted to Christianity and left it at that? No, he had to become a big mouth about it and run around shouting, "Look at what I experienced! Look how wonderful it was! Aren't I special?" And the rest, as they say, is history. Well, history for the nascent Western world, anyway.

A number of centuries later, it would culminate in the *Divine Comedy*. I remembered that I had actually once attempted to read the *Divine Comedy*, but I put it down soon after. It just didn't flow—not like a novel, anyway. All those lines of poetry wouldn't slide easily across the page from one line to the next. They broke off in all the wrong places. The mind and eye got confused, and you lost your place.

Ben said he had read it. No surprise there. What hadn't he read? He had clearly read more books than I had ever dreamed of reading. But didn't I have a right to feel just a little proud of myself? Sure, maybe I hadn't taken any philosophy courses in college to speak of—other than that basic Introduction to Logic course—and maybe I hadn't read all the philosophy books Ben had read. But still, I had responded to his *Cosmic Consciousness* book report with a few thoughtful and unique insights of my own, hadn't I? He agreed with my imaginative fleshing out of C.M.C. and my point about whether good weather influenced her cosmic consciousness experience.

I wondered how I had come up with that idea in the first place. I didn't remember analyzing my way to it—not in the rigorous way Ben did, going through each case of cosmic consciousness and arriving at his own conclusions. I had no idea where the idea had come from. It just popped into my head. Like a flash. It was my own realization, and a good one, too, if I did say so myself. That was proven by the fact that Ben just didn't dismiss it outright or laugh it off. He had to think about it and deal with it. He had to admit that it was something to be factored in.

But you had to respect him. Ben knew what he was after, and he was making headway. He had found the *Cosmic Consciousness* book, and it confirmed he was on the right path. Even though he found holes in the text, he also found corroboration in it. Cosmic consciousness—the big realization—really existed. People like Plotinus, Yepes, Behmen, Carpenter, and especially C.M.C. had experienced it. And they had written about it. They told you what to expect—what it was like. Ben had set his mind to it, and he would undoubtedly get there.

I started to think about myself. Was I making headway? Was I getting somewhere? I remembered that tomorrow was Sunday, which meant it was time to check the Help Wanted ads again. Would there finally be an ad in there that would be a good fit for me? A job where I could make some real money?

I began to imagine myself working for a big corporation with a decent salary, health benefits, and a company car. My life would be completely different. Who knows where I would end up?

I continued to think like this until I fell, asleep.

7 Ben's Dream

If someone says they intend to be President of the United States someday, don't ask them about it the next time you run into them. Don't call them on the phone and ask what progress they've made. Don't knock on their door and say, "How's it going?" or "What's new?"

Why? Because they might interpret those ordinary greetings the wrong way. They might think you're pressuring them, needling them, or even mocking them. When someone has set their sights on a grand or preposterous goal, the best policy is to give them lots of space. Asking them what progress they've made—no matter how innocently you ask them that—isn't going to help them, and most likely will either cause them to explode or to make them feel like a failure. Someone who's dreaming doesn't like to be woken up.

That was my thinking anyway. So all through the next week—after my long session with Ben, when he reviewed the *Cosmic Consciousness* book and declared that he was going to find a way to experience cosmic consciousness himself—I minded my own business. I went to Computer Connection every day and suffered through my soul-draining shift. When I came home I took my beer glass from the cupboard and put it in the freezer. I got out of my monkey-suit and slipped into clothes more fit for a human being. Soon I was drinking my ice-cold beer and meditating on my life in light of the day's events. Then I heated up a TV dinner which I ate while watching an old movie on television. That was basically my regimen every day of the work week.

On Saturday, I did my errands, which consisted of getting groceries and doing laundry. After that, I roller-skated in Golden Gate Park, listening to the drum-beating music of The Cars on my Walkman cassette player. I went all the way to Ocean Beach and back. That gave me plenty of exercise.

On Sunday, I scoured the Help Wanted ads for a new job. As usual, most of them called for experience in sales areas where I had no background, such as pharmaceuticals, manufacturing, or insurance. However, there was an ad from Hewlett-Packard seeking computer sales representatives. Unfortunately, it said they preferred applicants with an MBA degree, as well as knowledge of major computing languages. That ruled me out. I could only hope that next Sunday's newspaper would be better.

I began the next week just like the last: minding my own business and following my daily regimen—work, home, beer, TV dinner, movie, bed. But when the middle of the week came and I hadn't run into Ben, I started to worry. He knew when I normally got home from work. Why hadn't he coincidentally been in the lobby? Why hadn't he opened his door as I was going up the stairs and invited me in for a cup of tea? I began to think of excuses I could use to knock on his door and not have him interpret what I said the wrong way. I could say I wanted his advice on something. But what? Perhaps on how I could get a better job? No, he was an academic. Would he really know anything about the kind of job search I needed to do? Would he even know how someone might go about selling himself and getting ahead in the business world?

By the time Saturday rolled around, I couldn't stand the suspense and worry any longer. I decided I had to go down and knock on his door. My plan was simply to say, "I just wanted to say hi." That was the best I could come up with. But I had to go through with it—I wouldn't be able to rest unless I did.

I went down the stairs and knocked firmly, but not loudly, three times on his door. From inside, I heard Ben's voice asking who it was.

"It's me," I said, in my best nonchalant voice. "I just wanted to say hi."

"Come in, it's unlocked," was his reply.

I stepped in. Ben was sitting on the futon. The room was in semidarkness. His Venetian blinds were only slightly open, letting in thin bands of light. He looked preoccupied and uneasy. His usual confidence was gone. He looked at me with an uncertainty and seriousness I hadn't seen in him before. I worried he would say something like, "Okay, you've said hi—now please turn around and leave," since I was no doubt distracting him and keeping him from his "goal."

"Have you ever had a dream," he began in a low, quivering voice, "that seemed so real you felt that the world—the outside world—was affected by it?"

"Well, I… no, I don't think so," I stammered.

I sat down in the armchair across from him. I was so relieved he wasn't dismissing me that I went on talking.

"I have had some pretty crazy dreams in my time, though. Come to think of it, they're always pretty crazy. Normally, I can't remember them when I wake up—half the time, anyway. I—"

"I had a dream early this morning," he interrupted, "and I've been awake and sitting here ever since. I can't help thinking that something momentous has happened—that I've done something that's affected the world itself."

"With a dream? Why? What was the dream?"

"Like you, I'm used to having dreams that are often irrational and therefore easily forgotten, or because they're vague, almost impossible to remember. And then there are the dreams that *are* memorable, ones that fall into the wish-fulfillment category, dreams where I get what I'm trying to get, or wish I could get in my waking life. But the dream I had early this morning doesn't fit into any category I can think of."

He sat slouched on the futon as if he could feel the weight of the atmosphere bearing down on him.

I asked gingerly, "What exactly was the dream?"

"It was actually a short dream, now that I think of it. I've noticed that my mind often creates a dream world from our everyday waking world. It uses places I've been in my waking life—rooms, streets, backyards, fields, buildings—and objects I've seen—cars, trucks, buses, boats, bikes—and it uses those places and objects to create new, unusual places and things in the dream. But this dream happened right here in this room. I mean, it started in this room. I was chasing a small animal around—right here in this very room."

He motioned across the floor and around the room.

"It was like a small dog or large rodent. I was afraid it was going to bite me—I don't know exactly what it was. Then, very quickly, I chased it into the bathroom, and it hopped into the toilet. But before I could flush it down, it shot up, turning into a tall, flesh-gray pillar. It was as big as a whale, and for a moment, I thought it had a human face. But then, in one quick, instinctual motion, I stabbed it—right in its head, and it spurted blood. In the blink of an eye, it was sucked down into the toilet as quickly as it had burst out of it."

This entire time Ben had been looking past me. But now he stopped and peered into my eyes. Then he looked past me again.

"I've been feeling guilty ever since, but at the same time, heroic—guilty that I would mercilessly kill a living thing, but heroic that I would take such warrior-like action. It all happened so quickly, and it was all very instinctual and reflexive. No real thought was involved. I don't know where the knife or the sword came from. It just appeared in my hand."

He stopped talking abruptly, glanced at me, then went on.

"So this was a body and soul dream. That's the only category I can give it. I woke up wet with sweat, as if I had actually been physically exerting myself—chasing that thing around the room here and into the bathroom—and then smiting that gigantic creature."

He paused, thinking, then began again.

"I know I just said it was a body and soul dream, but I don't like that word *soul*. So, let's just say it was a mind-body dream—which is a completely new dream category for me. And I feel like it's had an effect on the real world that I can't explain. It's not logical, I know. Nevertheless, it's a very strange, powerful feeling."

"What kind of effect could it have had on the real world?"

"I don't know. I just feel that it did. Somehow, I don't know how. That's why I've just been sitting here. I don't want to go outside. I don't want to face the world after what I've done."

"Well, it was just a dream after all," I offered. "It's probably a mistake to take it too seriously."

Ben pierced me with his eyes.

"Normally, I would agree with you, but this one's different—as I said."

"Of course!" I answered quickly, worried that I had crossed a boundary. It was obvious that he was shaken by his dream, and I knew in that moment that it was wrong of me to trivialize it. I decided to remain silent.

A few minutes passed, and I was relieved when he finally spoke again. I felt as if he had forgiven me.

"Why would I have such a dream? I've been sitting here thinking about the sewer system it disappeared into. We're all connected through it, aren't we? Think about it. The entire city is linked by sewer pipes. They go under our locked doors right into our bathrooms in our apartments and homes. The only thing that keeps us from being directly connected to every other bathroom in this city is a gallon or two of water in our toilet bowls. A transparent liquid is the only thing that separates us from every other human being who lives in San Francisco. We are all physically joined through our plumbing. And this gray, shiny, huge, fish-like, human-like creature was sucked right down into that unseen network of pipes—like a ghost.

I have the strongest feeling that I actually killed a gigantic living creature, and I don't know why. But I had to do it. It was so quick—there was no thought involved. I feel like it really happened. Somehow, something has been affected in the external world. I feel like I truly killed something in the real world—not just in the dream. And I feel like something is still going to happen because of it. Some other shoe is going to drop."

I was tempted again to say, *Don't worry about it, it was just a dream*, but I caught myself.

"That's really a strange and powerful experience," I said, nodding. "I can see that now."

"Yes," Ben said, warming back up to me. "Experience doesn't just apply to the external world. It applies to the inner world too. Now I know what Jung meant when he said one of his patients *really* had been to the moon because she dreamed she traveled there and stood on its surface. Experience is something that relates to reality—inner and outer, mind and body—all reality."

"All reality?"

"When you look up at a tree and notice a branch swaying in a soft wind, that perception—that experience— is happening in you, isn't it? What's the difference if you look up at a tree in your dream and notice it swaying in a soft wind? It's still happening in you, isn't it?"

"Yes, I guess so, but—"

"It's still happening in you."

"But there's a difference, isn't there? One happens in the external world and one happens in the internal world?"

"Yes, that's a difference. But from our individual point of view, deep down, there is no difference—no ultimate difference. Both are experiences. Both are meaningful.

Meaning is the realm that unites both the inner and the outer worlds."

"I've never heard that before. I have to say, though, that sounds true enough."

Ben's eyes brightened.

"I don't think I've ever realized it that clearly before either."

"Sounds like a pretty big realization."

"It's a good realization, but not a big one," Ben said, correcting me.

"Sorry. But if you don't mind my asking, how exactly will you know when you have the big realization?"

"It won't come as an idea like meaning is the realm that unites both the inner and the outer worlds. It'll be like what happened to Bucke or C.M.C. For me, it has to come as an experience."

"Yes, of course. You explained that before."

"Don't get me wrong. A big insight like meaning is the realm that unites both the inner and the outer worlds is nothing to sneeze at. It's a great insight, if I do say so myself. And it may be an important ingredient that, when put together with other realizations, produces the big realization. I don't know. Time will tell."

"But how do you know that the dream you just had wasn't the big realization? Especially since you just said the inner and outer worlds are united in meaning and that both are based on experience. The way you're talking about your dream, and the effect it's having on you, certainly sounds like a big realization based on experience."

He looked at me, his face frozen. I could tell he was flustered. I confess, I had a secret moment of enjoyment at making him feel that way. He had philosophized himself into a paper bag, and now he couldn't get out of it.

"Michael, I have to be honest with you," he said finally. "I think you've stumped me. I don't have the words right now to answer your question. It's a fair question. It's an excellent question."

"I'm sorry, I wasn't intentionally trying to stump you. It just occurred to me, and I had to ask."

"There's no need to apologize. You've given me something to think about, and I appreciate that. All I can say right now is that I don't think this is *the* big realization—although it is a big experience. It's certainly different from Bucke's and the others. But I'm going to need some time to give you a better explanation."

Ben was very amiable and even offered to make me tea. I politely declined, explaining that I had my Saturday errands to run. He suggested that I stop by tomorrow when he might have a better explanation.

I stood up to leave, and he jumped up to open the door for me. I felt I had at least brought him out of his depressed state, and I felt good about that.

Sitting on my toilet that night, I couldn't help but imagine it being connected to a vertical pipe that dropped down from my floor, along with other pipes, down to a horizontal pipe under our building that ran into a larger pipe under Judah Street, where other pipes from other buildings connected to it, and where it was part of a big web of pipes that eventually came together in one large conduit that flowed to the sanitation facility at the Pacific Ocean near the San Francisco Zoo.

I imagined that I was the fish-god Glaucus, magically jumping into the toilet and swimming through the entire network of San Francisco's sewer pipes. I could pop up and out of anyone's toilet bowl I wanted to, look around, and disappear back into an endless network of pipes. I could even spring up and out of the toilet at Mayor Dianne Feinstein's house if I wished to—or even the toilet of that beautiful girl who had promenaded past Ben and me as we came out of Golden Gate Park.

I wondered why Ben was so interested in plumbing that it would appear in his dream. But then I thought about it and realized that I was just as interested in plumbing as he was. Plumbing, because we can't see it completely, is mysterious. Day in and day out, we use sinks, toilets, bathtubs, and showers. Who can help wondering—consciously or unconsciously—where exactly those pipes run beneath the floor and inside the walls? Every time I flush a toilet, there are those moments of suspense, waiting and wondering if it will go down or overflow. And if it doesn't, what an embarrassing mess that would be.

Mostly unseen, plumbing is one of those things that is part of our conscious and subconscious lives, day and night. I've never liked things I can't see. Pipes shouldn't be hidden under floors or behind walls. If I ever manage to own a home someday, I'd have the pipes installed out in the open, on the outside of the walls. And they would be transparent, because I want to see not only the pipes but also what flows through them. Who knows? Maybe someday, I might actually be able to own a house.

Tomorrow would be Sunday, and that meant the big, fat Sunday newspaper, with its Help Wanted ads, would be waiting for me outside my door in the hallway—the means to a bright and promising future dropped right on my doorstep.

All I had to do was bend down and pick it up.

8   A Dream's Reality

Sunday morning finally came. It was time to check the Help Wanted ads. I opened my door, bent down, and picked up the thick Sunday paper. I brought it in and plopped it on my kitchen table. Then I prepared my breakfast: coffee with cream, buttered toast, and a banana. Sitting at the table, I sipped my coffee and pulled the newspaper closer to scan the headlines. The main story was about President Reagan claiming that El Salvador was making progress on human rights. Another was about a Chinese tennis star seeking asylum in the United States.

When I turned the paper over to read the below-the-fold news, this headline grabbed my attention:

80 TONS OF DEAD WHALE IN S.F.

The black and white photo below the headline showed one person standing in the sand at the whale's head. Another stood in the shallow water at its midpoint. Two more were in waist-deep water at its tail. At the bottom of the photo was this caption:

Members of the Coastwatch Wildlife Society get help from surfers in measuring an adult male whale that washed ashore near Fort Funston Beach in San Francisco. The 80-foot, 80-ton mammal may have died up to three weeks ago, experts said. The smelly carcass washed ashore belly up and drew a small crowd of onlookers. (Story, B-1)

Even though I hadn't experienced Ben's dream with all its emotional intensity, the correspondence to what Ben had dreamt jumped out at me. Just a coincidence? No way. There was the huge, gray, whale-like creature that Ben had stabbed and watched as it was sucked down the toilet. Then there was his conviction that what he had done had actually affected the real world. And now, the very next day, here was this photo of a gigantic gray whale lying on Fort Funston Beach near San Francisco's sewage plant. This couldn't just be a coincidence.

I immediately wondered if I should show the paper with its surreal headline to Ben. How would he take it? No doubt it would shock him even more than it had shocked me.

He would at least see it as proof that his dream was indeed bound up with reality—that one's inner life is fundamentally connected to the outer world. Hadn't he said meaning is the realm that unites the inner and the outer, the subjective and the objective, the mind and the body? But what if he interpreted it to mean even more than that?

He was already engaged in what most people would consider a very unusual personal mission, wasn't he? Trying to get to the root of reality? Trying to reach the stars by getting to the bottom of things? Wanting to be like religious figures or great thinkers of the past—people who were so exceptional that they were recorded in history books, so that their life stories and accomplishments could be passed down from one generation to the next?

What if he saw the whale as proof that he had some kind of superpower? Hadn't he repeated a number of times that he feared his actions in his dream had affected the world itself? Couldn't this be read as confirmation of that? But where would it lead him? Over some mental edge? Would he lose all sense of proportion? Would he forgo that healthy balance of skepticism and belief that is the mainstay of a healthy mind? If I showed him this news story, wouldn't that be like throwing gasoline on the fire in his mind? Would he go extreme on me? Would I be helping him become psychotic?

Was that even the right word to use?

I ran into the other room. Kneeling down, I pulled out my Big Dic. I cracked it open—right to the P section. Was that a coincidence? My fingers trembled as I flipped through pages until I found the word psychotic. But its definition only referred me to psychosis. When I found my way to that word, it was just as I feared: *psychosis* meant a person experiencing an impaired contact with reality. Wasn't that exactly the territory Ben was venturing into?

I closed my Big Dic and got up. I stood staring out my window, past the wrought-iron fire escape, into the bit of the street that I could see below. Suddenly I realized that Ben had the paper delivered to his door, just like me. Should I go down and grab the paper before he had a chance to pick it up himself? After that, I could take my time deciding if and when I would show it to him. Yes, I decided, that was the best course of action to take.

I rushed out of my apartment and stepped quietly down the stairs. But when I got within view of Ben's apartment, my heart sank. I didn't see a paper lying in front of his door.

Now I had a decision to make. Should I knock on his door or just forget about the whole thing? But if I knocked, I could find out if he had already seen the paper. Lots of people bring it in and let it sit for days, or they just look at the part that interests them, like the sports section or the TV listings. If he hadn't seen or read the article about the whale, I could come up with an excuse for needing to borrow his copy. I could say that mine wasn't delivered and that I wanted to check the Help Wanted ads. Then I could take the paper and figure out what to do later.

I knocked on the door.

"Come in, Michael," Ben's voice called from inside.

I opened the door and stepped in.

"How did you know it was me?"

"I just knew," Ben said, smiling.

He was sitting on the futon like yesterday, but he wasn't slouched. His eyes were bright and confident. The blinds were up, letting in plenty of early morning sunlight through the window. The Sunday morning paper lay before him on the coffee table.

He saw me look at it as I sat down in the armchair.

"What do you think?" he asked, observing me.

"About what?" I answered, unable to hide my grin.

"You know what."

"Actually, if you don't mind, I would like to know what you think about it," I said, blushing.

"Have you read the article?"

"No, I only saw the photo on the front page and read the caption."

"Then, I think it would be a good idea for you to read the whole article before we talk about it, don't you?"

"Yes, of course. Yes."

Ben pushed the newspaper in my direction.

"Feel free to make comments or ask questions as you read through it."

"I will," I said, taking the paper.

Ben sat back, concealing a yawn with his hand.

The caption on the front page said the story was on page B-1, so I unfolded the newspaper on my lap and found the B section.

"Okay, it says here the whale washed ashore Saturday morning."

"That's when I had my dream," Ben said calmly. "It was yesterday morning, so it's roughly in sync with it washing ashore."

"Yes, that's correct. But it also says here that the whale was dead for as long as three weeks."

"Yes, I read that too. But I don't think details like that are important in these cases. The meaningful thing is that it washed up on the beach around the same time I was having my dream."

"In that case, I think I should tell you something that this article isn't mentioning."

"What's that?"

"The San Francisco sewage plant is near Fort Funston Beach, where the whale washed up."

Ben's eyes widened.

"Really? Okay, now that's certainly significant, don't you think?"

"Yes, there's no denying it. That fact struck me when I saw the photo and read the caption before I came down here. Shall I go on?"

"Yes, please do."

I skimmed the article for more details.

"It was spotted floating near the Farallon Islands last week… It's an adult male, 76 to 80 feet long, and weighs as much as 80 tons… Indications are that it is a blue whale… Blue whales are the largest animals on Earth… Hang on—the rest of the story is on page B-4."

I turned the pages of the newspaper on my lap and located the conclusion to the story.

"The Coastwatch vet didn't know what killed the whale… but said typical causes for whale deaths are shooting, shark attacks, entanglement in fishing nets, disease, and parasites… Coastwatch workers were going to return to the beach after midnight during low tide hours to examine the whale's skull."

"So, that means they were there in the early hours of this morning," Ben said, pondering aloud. "I wonder why they want to examine the whale's skull. I do remember stabbing the creature high up near its head in my dream."

"Yes, I remember you saying that, too."

"Well, what do you think about all this?"

"It's surreal. You just had a dream about killing a whale-like thing that disappears down your toilet, and then the very next day there's this story about a dead whale that washed up on the beach near the San Francisco sewage plant. That's an incredible coincidence, that's for sure."

"Except that *coincidence* isn't the right word."

"You're right. So, what is the right word?"

"Synchronicity. It's synchronicity. As Jung says, a coincidence is a random event that doesn't really mean anything. But a coincidence that's full of meaning—that's a special kind of coincidence, and he called it *synchronicity*. It's certainly synchronicity for me, anyway."

"No, you're right. Coincidence isn't the right word."

"Well, I have to see this whale for myself," Ben said adamantly. "I intend to go to the beach to see it. You're welcome to come with me—if you want to, that is."

Ben was his old self again. He knew what he wanted. He stared at me with those same piercing eyes from when I first met him in front of the mailboxes in our lobby. That was when he asked me if I really liked my job. I was relieved that he was looking at this whole thing philosophically and not psychotically. It made me want to help him. Besides, I had never seen a beached whale before, and since it was Sunday, I hadn't really planned on doing anything in particular, anyway. Well, except for studying the Help Wanted ads. But I could do that later.

I glanced back down at the article.

"Okay, well, it says no attempt will be made to move the whale while they continue investigating, so it should still be there. It washed ashore near Fort Funston Beach. We could easily catch a streetcar from here, then transfer to a bus at Sunset Boulevard to get to the San Francisco Zoo. From there, I believe it's about a twenty-minute hike."

I looked toward the window.

"A walk on the beach would be nice. It's certainly a good day for it."

"It certainly is." Ben nodded.

I suggested we break off and get ready for our trip to see the mysterious whale. Ben agreed and was pleased that I would be going with him.

A half-hour later we walked out of our apartment building and down the block to the streetcar stop at 9th and Judah. We caught the N Judah to Sunset Boulevard where, after a short wait, we boarded a bus to the San Francisco Zoo. From there, we walked along the beach, heading south toward Fort Funston Beach. The air was warm and the sky was clear blue, except for a few wisps of white clouds. After about ten minutes, we passed the massive, bunker-like concrete facade that marks the entrance to the San Francisco sewage plant. The plant itself is not visible, as it is built into the hillside. Gray concrete walls slope away from the huge gated opening—a gaping maw for large trucks.

"I think you could definitely get a whale in and out of there," Ben quipped.

We trudged through the sand along the beach for another five minutes or so, when we discerned a crowd of people in the distance, standing around what seemed to be a dark gray, sloping mound. A pungent, stinky smell suddenly invaded our nostrils.

"Do you smell that?" I exclaimed. "That's really disgusting—like rotten eggs and rotten fish at the same time."

Ben didn't say anything. He kept his eyes on the hulking gray mass that was coming into focus as a huge dead whale—a gigantic presence that was no longer an idea or a photo in the newspaper, but a palpable reality.

When we reached the whale, Ben found an unoccupied spot and stood with his shoe tips almost touching the whale's slimy, shimmering skin. He stood for a while, thinking. Then he walked to the front of the whale. I followed and stood beside him.

After a moment, he pointed with his hand, flat like a fin, toward the whale's head.

"Do you see that? His head is wounded. I stabbed that thing in the head—do you remember?"

"Yes, and then you said it was sucked down into the toilet. But you know, there are probably many reasons for its head to be damaged like that."

"Such as?"

"Like the newspaper said, things such as fishing nets."

"I can't believe a net could do that to a whale's head."

"No, probably not. Still, it could have been hit by a ship or attacked by a shark. Or maybe it ran into jagged rocks."

Ben looked up and down the beach.

"I don't see any rocks or outcroppings here."

"No, that's true," I admitted.

"It's weird, isn't it? I'm standing here between two worlds. I know all this can be explained in the external, cause-and-effect world, but it can also be explained by what I did in my dream."

"Is that what's called a dilemma?"

Ben thought for a moment.

"No, a dilemma is having to choose between two difficult courses of action. This is a kind of co-explication—a strange mental interchangeability. If there's a word for it, I can't think of it right now. But I can tell you this: it's an uncanny state of mind. My consciousness is oscillating between these two different standpoints."

"So is this a big experience you're having? Is it cosmic consciousness?"

"Oh, that gets us back to yesterday, doesn't it? And I said I would have an explanation for you, didn't I?"

"Yes, about whether your dream qualifies as a big experience of the cosmic consciousness kind. I guess we can add what you're experiencing right now to that, too."

"Well, I think I just gave you the explanation. It's a very peculiar state of mind. So, my answer is: no. My dream was a powerful, eye-opening experience—but it was not cosmic consciousness. And what I just described to you isn't a cosmic consciousness experience, either. It's a weirdly powerful experience, yes. But just like those individuals in the *Cosmic Consciousness* book who had intense experiences—whether they were mystical visions, religious conversions, or moral awakenings—just as I said their experiences weren't examples of cosmic consciousness, I now have to say the same about my dream and this synchronicity experience: they are not cosmic consciousness experiences."

I nodded. "I guess that settles that. So, are you ready to head back?"

"I am."

We both took one last look at the dead whale, then walked back up the beach to the San Francisco Zoo, where we caught the bus to the N Judah streetcar, which took us back to 9th and Judah.

Ben insisted on buying me lunch, so we walked down to the Pot and Pan on 9th Avenue and ordered egg rolls and hot and sour soup. We shared a smile as we watched the waitress pour the tea into our small, white, handleless teacups.

As we strolled back up to our apartment building, I decided I no longer needed to worry about Ben's state of mind, and that I could now ask him about his progress in trying to experience cosmic consciousness.

I didn't feel he would get angry, and I very much doubted that my question would demoralize him, either.

"What are you going to do now? I mean, about trying to experience cosmic consciousness."

"I've been thinking about that too," he replied. "I can't help but feel that my whale dream—my body dream—aside from the obvious sexual connotations, was also a message, a clue from my unconscious."

"How so?"

"Because it made me realize something."

"Which was?"

"That I've been trying to experience cosmic consciousness by *thinking* my way there. I've been putting my mind over my body. But the body includes the mind, doesn't it? The mind is embodied. If that's true, then why not let my body lead me to cosmic consciousness? So—no more trying to think my way there. No more believing that the mixing of ideas in the big container of my mind will lead to a big explosion, to a big realization. Now, I'm going to try the opposite. Now, I'm going to try not thinking at all."

"Not thinking at all? But how can you do that?"

"Through yoga meditation."

"Yoga meditation? Really?"

"Yes, it worked for Saint Yepes—I mean, Saint John of the Cross—and Behmen too, didn't it? Yoga is the intentional stopping of the spontaneous activity of the mind-stuff."

"Wait, what? Is that what yoga is?"

"If I'm not mistaken, that's what Patanjali says it is in his *Yoga Sutras*. Or something like that anyway."

"That sounds scary. Almost dangerous. If you stop your mind from thinking, what if it doesn't start up again?"

"I'm not worried about that happening." Ben chuckled.

"If you *think* so," I said with a laugh.

"Anyway, as I see it," Ben went on, "yoga is the quieting of the mind, so the body and the unconscious can take over. It's the complete opposite of thinking."

"Well, that's an approach you haven't tried before, so why not give it a try? Now that I think about it, meditation is kind of like doing nothing, isn't it? So, come to think of it, maybe you have tried it before. Maybe, without knowing it, you were on the right track the first day I met you."

"You're right!" Ben laughed. "I didn't even think of that. Well, I'm certainly going to try it now."

We had reached the doors of our apartment building. Still chuckling, I unlocked the door. We walked in and stepped up the ten arabesque-tiled stairs, past the shiny brown plaster lions, to the upper lobby floor. We said our goodbyes and went our separate ways. Ben slipped into his apartment, and I climbed the stairs to mine.

When I entered my apartment, I saw the Sunday *Chronicle* lying on my kitchen table. I had forgotten all about it. But now my anticipation and excitement returned. Was this the day that I would find a Help Wanted ad that would change my life?

I shut the door and went over to the table. The paper was still lying there just as I had left it, with the side showing Ben's whale photo facing up.

I cleared the table, quickly opened the paper to the Help Wanted section, and started my search.

As usual, I could ignore the large sales ads at the bottom of the page for pharmaceuticals, manufacturing, and insurance sales reps.

I felt a flush of excitement when I saw an ad for a Corporate Sales Trainee. Unfortunately, they wanted a year of outside sales experience. How could I talk my way around that? Plus, it was through an employment agency, and they didn't name the corporation that they were fronting for. Understandable—but still.

There were numerous other sales ads for everything from vitamins and fine art to fashion eyewear, paper products, real estate, and more. But then my eyes landed on this:

HELP WANTED
SALES

3M COMPANY

We are interviewing for experienced professional major accounts reps, to call on customer and prospects in the Bay Area. Business machines or copier sales exper. preferred. College degree is a plus. Salary + bonus, co. car. & excel. fringe benefits. Send resume to G. Wells, 3M Business Products Sales Center, Rincon Annex. Box 3996, S.F. Ca. 94119. Equal Opportunity Employer

Now, that's what I called promising. I didn't have experience as an experienced major account rep, nor did I have experience in business machines or copier sales, but I did have experience in computer sales. And weren't computers going to be the business machines of the future? What's more, I did have a college degree, which the ad said was a plus. There was certainly enough in this ad to give me hope. It wasn't a perfect match, but it was close enough for me to give it a go. At the very least, it would test my innate sales skills. Computer Connection had taught me to sell myself, the store, and the solution. Why not try to sell myself to the 3M Company as the solution to their problem of needing a sales representative?

This was definitely an ad I had to respond to. This was an interview I had to get. I went into the other room, grabbed my portable typewriter, and brought it back to the kitchen table. In short order, I fired off a cover letter saying that I thought my BA degree and recent computer sales experience qualified me for the account representative position with 3M. I explained that such a position would require an energetic and outgoing person—qualities that I possessed. I also noted that, as a computer salesman for Computer Connection, I had gained valuable inside and outside sales experience, and that most of my clients had been bankers, lawyers, corporate executives, and small business owners.

I indicated that, even though my home phone number appeared on my resume, it might be easier to contact me at Computer Connection, and I included that number.

I ended by writing: "Looking forward to hearing from you, I remain," followed by the standard closing "Sincerely yours," my signature, and an "Enc: resume" below that.

I typed the addresses on the envelope and slid my cover letter and resume into it. After licking the adhesive, I pressed it closed and applied the stamp. Then, I leaned the letter against the bottom of my apartment door so I wouldn't forget to mail it Monday morning on my way to work.

Later that night, when it was time to enjoy my beer, I must have tipped the can the wrong way, because the foam filled half the glass. I had to wait a while before I could pour more. When I did—pouring slowly this time—the foam puffed up again, threatening to overflow the rim.

I don't like a lot of beer foam. I like the liquid. I watched and waited patiently as pinholes appeared in the foam while it began to shrink. After a while, the foam mostly transformed itself back into my cold, golden beer. Now that's what I like—transformation I can see with my own eyes. That's something I can get behind and experience every day. Perhaps someday I'll want to experience the transformation Ben was looking for. But for the time being, white foam turning into liquid golden goodness was good enough for me.

Later, as I was lying in bed, I remembered the name that Ben had mentioned: Patanjali. Once again, I wished I had a personal computer to make it easier to find out more about him. I scolded myself for being too proud to ask Ben to tell me more about the guy.

Although it sounded dangerous, I wondered how a person could go about stopping the mind-stuff. It would certainly make life easier when it was time to go to sleep.

9 Ben's Yoga Meditation

On Monday morning, when I saw the streetcar coming up Judah Street, I turned and rushed down 9th Avenue to the little storefront post office near 9th and Irving. I deposited my letter to 3M into a blue mailbox out front. Then, I scrambled over to the streetcar, now at the 9th and Irving stop, and managed to step inside just as the doors were closing.

I like sitting on the streetcar on the way to work. That's when you can enjoy just being alive. There's a sense of accomplishment just in sitting there. You feel you have a right to be complacent because you can't really get up and do anything else. You're getting to work—you're accomplishing something—so you don't feel guilty about just letting time pass. That's when you can live in the moment, enjoying the changing view outside while observing the people who are getting in and out.

Mailing the letter also gave me a sense of achievement and put me in a good mood that stayed with me throughout the day.

When an elderly man wandered into the store, I could tell right away that he was the curious type and not a real prospect. But I didn't mind. I felt no pressure to avoid him or be stingy with my time. I didn't need to discriminate between a profitable and an unprofitable encounter. I was like the character Sydney Greenstreet played in *Casablanca*—giving advice to the young refugee couple while wondering why he was doing it, since it couldn't possibly profit him.

The inquisitive old man must have sensed that I was open to him because he walked straight over to me.

"Can you tell me how they work?" he asked, gesturing to the computer beside me.

"Happy to," I answered cheerfully.

I popped the lid off the Apple II Plus so he could look inside.

"Atoms of electricity flow through all these thin strips of solder and small square chips," I explained. "They're like infinitesimal squirrels running at lightning speed through countless miniature mazes and station stops. Every turn or stop-and-go they make creates binary bits of information. In other words, data—like numbers or letters of the alphabet."

"That's amazing," the old man said.

He stared down into the computer for a while longer. Scratching the thin hair on his head, he looked up at me with gratitude. Then, he thanked me, turned, and wandered out of the store.

I felt that same goodwill and generosity—that willingness to freely give of my time—for the rest of the week. You have to earn the hopefulness that frees you to enjoy just being alive. Mailing that letter, which could change my life, opened up a whole new outlook on the world for me. It allowed me to enjoy each moment of the day because I felt empowered. I had achieved something. Something was in the works. Maybe I'd get the job, maybe

I wouldn't—but at least I was taking action. If this one didn't work out, there would always be the Help Wanted ads next Sunday. I was sure I would eventually find a similar ad and could apply again.

Of course, my lighthearted feeling was mostly based on anticipating a positive response to my resume. At times, I had to tell myself that it was possible that I wouldn't hear from 3M and that I probably wouldn't even get an interview. But the antidote to that fear was that there would most likely be more ads like that one—and that I was on my way.

My optimism was justified on Friday morning when Janet, the store's front-counter manager, called out to me from behind her cash register, saying that I had a phone call. I walked up to the counter, and she handed me the phone. It was a man from 3M. They were interested in me and wanted to meet. We arranged for an interview on Tuesday. Needless to say, I was elated. My positive thinking had paid off.

When I woke up Saturday morning, I decided it was time to check in with Ben. After breakfast, I went down and knocked on his door. I heard Ben say, "Hang on" from inside. After a few moments, he opened the door and invited me in. Once I sat down, I told him the news: I had answered a Help Wanted ad for a better job at a major corporation and was going to an interview on Tuesday.

He looked straight into me with his probing eyes. The room seemed to grow quiet and slightly darken behind him.

"Is that what you really want to do?" he asked.

"Well, not exactly," I replied. "But I don't think I can do what I really want to do—not at this point in my life, anyway."

"I understand," he said benevolently. "That's all right then. I hope you get the job."

"So how are your meditations going?" I asked, changing the subject.

He shrugged.

"I don't know exactly. Nothing big has happened yet."

"Well, you've never meditated before, have you? Aren't you supposed to get a guru or something, so you learn to do it the right way?"

"My instinct is not to get a guru. That just isn't in me. But I did get a book that backs me up on that."

He picked up a small reddish-brown paperback from the coffee table and handed it to me. Its title was *How to Meditate: The Acclaimed Guide to Self-Discovery*. In the center of the cover was the silhouette of a small tree against a square background. Silhouettes of larger trees, each set against larger square backgrounds, were replicated behind it. It was to make you feel as if the small tree in the center were pulsating inward and outward, drawing you in while coming forward to meet you at the same time.

"This book says it's all right to try meditating on your own without getting a guru?" I asked.

"Yes, but I would have done that even if it had said otherwise."

A beeping sound interrupted us. Ben got up from the futon and walked over to a rug in the middle of the room. He pushed a button on the timer to stop the beeping, then came back and sat down.

"What's that for?"

"It's just a timer I use when I meditate," he explained. "That way I don't have to think about things. Like how long I've been meditating, that sort of thing."

"You say you don't want to think about things, but even if you're not thinking about time or keeping track of time, aren't you still thinking about something? When you're meditating, aren't you meditating on something? And doesn't that mean you're *thinking* about something?"

"No. When you meditate, you're *focusing* on something. You're stopping yourself from thinking by concentrating on it. You're focusing on your breathing or the whitish screen of your mind. So, you're really just listening to something or looking at something—or both. Thinking means your thoughts are changing—one thought following the next. But when you're meditating, when you're focusing on your breathing or your inner mental screen, your thoughts aren't really changing. You're not really thinking. You're just becoming one with an inner perception. That's how I do it, anyway. When I meditate on the blank white screen in my mind, my mind doesn't move like it does when I'm thinking. It stands still. It's not trying to figure something out. It's not thinking about the future or the past. It's in the present. It's still. Just observing—inwardly. Sort of like the tree on the cover of this book."

"Could you do it with your eyes open?"

"I don't see why not. Sure. Just focus on something."

He pointed with his finger.

"This chair or that rug. Just look at that, just stare at that. Yes, that's a form of meditation. Why not?"

We were both silent for a while. Then another question came to me.

"So what's the experience like?"

"It's relaxing, of course. But there haven't been any big realizations. Still, there was something that happened just the other day. It wasn't a realization, not a new experience in the strict sense of the word."

"What was it then?"

"I fell outside of time. Completely. My consciousness disappeared. It turned off like a light bulb."

"What do you mean? How could you even know that? If your consciousness turned off and turned back on, how would you even know that?"

"I was using the timer."

"Oh right, the timer."

"Normally, I've always felt when the timer went off, something like an hour had gone by. But yesterday, when I started meditating, I felt a sense of time passing for a little while—but then suddenly, the timer went off. So I must have shut off my mind completely. Just like when you're asleep. But I hadn't gone to sleep. I know that."

On my lunch break Monday, I walked up to the Business Branch of the San Francisco Public Library on Kearney Street to study the *Moody's* and the *Standard & Poor's* annual reports on 3M. I noted that it had a gross income of six billion dollars and 87,000 employees. They were in Abrasives, Chemicals, Photography, Printing, Recording Tape, Advertising, Health, and Consumer Products. I jotted it all down so I could mention those facts if the interviewer asked me if I knew anything about the company.

On Tuesday, I called in sick and took a bus to the Stonestown shopping center. Then I transferred to a San Mateo County bus to get to the Serramonte Center shopping area in Daly City. From there, I walked a block to the Serramonte Plaza business buildings, where the 3M Business Products Sales Center's suite of offices was located.

With my first interviewer, the topic of references came up. Since I didn't really have any references to speak of, I was tempted to mention my knowing a certain college philosophy professor. Luckily, I remembered what my grandmother once told me: *It's not what you say in an interview, it's what you don't say*. Because why, in God's name, would a sales manager be impressed with an obsessed philosopher who was trying to have a metaphysical experience? What was I thinking?

Instead, I settled for telling him that I couldn't really ask my current employer to vouch for me, could I? I worried that that would ruin my chances, but he seemed to understand. As it turns out, salespeople aren't sticklers for that sort of thing. They just want to know if you can persuade people. After all, I wasn't applying for a government job as an engineer or a scientist.

I thought the interviews went well. When I got home, I immediately composed a follow-up letter thanking Mr. Frank Price for the interesting and informative interview and for arranging the second interview with Mr. Gary McCartan.

I wrote that I was very impressed with the way things were done at 3M, as well as the diversity of the company's product line. I added that 3M was certainly a company for which I would be proud to work.

On Wednesday morning, I dropped my follow-up letter into one of the blue mailboxes in front of the little storefront post office near 9th and Irving. Then I walked over to the streetcar stop and caught the N Judah to Computer Connection.

When Saturday morning came, I visited Ben and told him I felt my interviews had gone well. He said he would keep his fingers crossed for me.

When I asked him how his meditations were going, he handed me a thick, bright red paperback book he said he had been studying:

The Serpent Power
The Secrets of
Tantric and Shaktic Yoga
Arthur Avalon
(Sir John Woodroffe)

The cover featured a colorful cartoon figure of a man seated in the lotus position, with six circular, flower-like symbols running up the center of his body. These little "blossoms" were surrounded by two spiraling cords, which reminded me of the DNA double helix symbol. On his head, he wore a close-fitting hairnet that looked like a swimming cap.

"What are those badges positioned along the guy's spine supposed to mean?" I asked, handing the book back to him.

Ben sighed, smiling.

"Those badges, as you call them, represent lotus flowers. They're known as *chakras*, which means wheels. They are the energy centers of the *kundalini*, the serpent power."

"Hence the name of the book?"

"Exactly. All these chakras are metaphors for the transformation of consciousness. They represent, in mythological symbols, what your psychological experience will be like at that level and what it means. This kind of yoga, kundalini yoga, sees your spiritual energy as coiled up like a serpent at the base of your spine. The person practicing this kind of yoga is supposed to arouse that serpent—that energy—so that it will awaken and travel up your spinal cord to reach this point."

Ben tapped the man's head.

"What's with the hairnet?" I asked, almost frowning.

Ben sighed again.

"That's the thousand-petalled lotus. In this drawing, it may look like a hairnet, but if you look closely at those little divisions in the hairnet, as you call it, you will see that those are petals—lotus flower petals."

I leaned in to take a closer look.

"Oh, yes, I can see that now. They look somewhat like big tear drops."

"It's known as the crown chakra because it sits on the top of your head. Coaxing the energy to rise all the way up to that level is the goal of this yoga. I believe that if I can get my spinal energy to rise there, I will experience cosmic consciousness."

"What makes you think that?"

"It's obvious just by looking at this illustration. But besides that, there are a number of times in this book where it actually says so."

Ben opened the book to a page he had marked with a Post-it note.

"This is from page five: *...the conduit for the force which is the arousing of the Devi called Kundalini the cosmic power in bodies...*"

He turned to another page on which he had placed a Post-it.

"This is from page thirty-four: *Nada is the first produced movement in ideating cosmic consciousness...*"

"Ideating? What does *ideating* mean?"

"It means forming ideas."

"And what does *nada* mean? I assume it isn't Spanish."

"You assume correctly. Nada is a special sound. I don't understand much about it myself, but it is somehow involved with cosmic consciousness. In any case, there are more places in this book where cosmic consciousness is mentioned."

"This serpent power yoga book… is it as big a find for you as the *Cosmic Consciousness* book was?"

"It certainly is," Ben said. "Maybe even more so."

All next week I was on pins and needles. Every day when I got home from work, I anxiously opened up my mailbox, hoping that an offer letter from 3M would be inside.

I had sent my follow-up letter on Wednesday, so I knew it was unlikely that an offer letter would arrive as early as

Monday. Still, when I opened my mailbox on Monday, I couldn't help hoping to see it there.

Of course, it wasn't.

I couldn't really say I felt real disappointment because it was unreasonable for me to think it really could have been there. The earliest they could have gotten my follow-up letter was Thursday. Still, couldn't they have made a decision on Thursday and gotten an offer letter off to me by Friday? But if they had already decided they wanted me, why would they have needed to wait for a follow-up letter from me at all? For all I knew maybe they *had* sent an offer letter out on Wednesday. So it wasn't entirely unreasonable to hope that an offer letter might be waiting for me in my mailbox on Monday.

On Tuesday, I thought I might reasonably expect the offer letter. Wasn't it likely—all things considered—that they would have sent it out on Monday? Wasn't it possible that it could reach me the next day? After all, it was only coming from Daly City, a contiguous suburb of San Francisco. But, of course, it wasn't there.

By Wednesday, I felt I was being more than reasonable to expect that the offer letter was waiting for me in the mailbox. Come on!—it *had* to be Wednesday. Even if they had received my follow-up letter on Monday, that gave them two full days to get their offer letter in the mail.

But it was not to be. When I opened my mailbox on Wednesday after work, it was completely empty—not even junk mail. I was disappointed, and now, clearly I had a right to be. But then, my hopes revived because I hadn't gotten a rejection letter, had I? No, I hadn't.

Okay, obviously I just didn't know how major corporations work. They take their time. They want to be sure. There's no way I was the only applicant. No doubt they had a lot of interviewees to consider. Who was I?—probably just one of many. I felt I had made a good impression, but maybe others had too. Maybe some had more sales experience than I did. Maybe they even had copier sales experience, which the ad said was preferred. My hopes took a dive.

On Thursday, I fully prepared myself to receive a rejection letter. There would be the standard phrases: *your qualifications were not a match for the position; we are sorry to say we cannot offer you a position at this time*, etc., etc. So when I put the key in and opened the little mailbox, I was relieved to see that there was nothing inside. An empty mailbox meant no rejection letter.

Part of me insisted that no rejection letter meant there could still be a chance that I would get an offer letter. I immediately scolded myself for thinking that, though. I was deluding myself. I was being silly. I needed to be realistic. If they truly wanted me, wouldn't they have rushed an offer letter to me? I had to be mature about this. There were always the Sunday Help Wanted ads, and Sunday was less than three days away.

When Friday came, I opened the mailbox. My heart sank when I saw a business-size envelope inside. The return address was 3M Company. So my rejection letter had finally arrived. That was it. It was over. There was no need to open it there in the mailbox area of the lobby. I simply took the letter in hand, shuffled up the stairs, and disappeared into my apartment. I dropped the letter on the kitchen table and went into the other room to get out of my monkey suit.

But then I turned around. Who was I kidding? I had to know for sure. I had to take it like a man. I marched back into the kitchen and picked up the letter. I slid the tip of my index finger into the gap under the seal flap and pushed it along, breaking the dried adhesive. I pulled out the letter and quickly skimmed for words:

happy to....................offer you...............
.............................$18K....................bonus...
..................benefits.........company car......

It was everything the ad had promised. I got the job! I almost yelled it out loud. Every cell in my body was clapping. I couldn't contain myself—I had to tell someone.

I rushed out of my apartment and down the stairs to Ben's door. I knocked louder than usual. Ben opened the door and looked at me with a puzzled expression on his face.

"I've got something really big to tell you!" I exclaimed.

"I'm all ears," Ben said.

"I just got the job offer letter from 3M Company!"

Ben's eyes brightened.

"Well, that's great! That's really great. I'm so happy for you. Things are really starting to go your way."

I thanked him for being so happy for me. Then I excused myself, saying I really needed to get back upstairs and out of my monkey suit. I told him it was going to be a two-beer night. What the hell—why not let Dionysus have his way with me? Maybe I'd make it a three-beer night.

He laughed and smiled at me.

My last day at Computer Connection was uneventful. There weren't any warm or memorable farewells. Janet, from behind the front counter, said goodbye to me rather matter-of-factly. No one else really noticed. That's how it was. Everyone was worried about their own future and how they could get out of that place and get a better job themselves.

One really wasn't inclined to nurture close friendships in a place like that. Other salespeople were your competitors. There was only so much foot traffic on the floor, only so many opportunities to find real sales prospects. When someone left, that meant there was one less person you had to worry about snagging the few real prospects that came into the store before you could.

At the same time, you were full of envy that they were moving on to a brighter future and leaving you behind in the retail sweatshop that was Computer Connection. How can you truly be happy for someone who was escaping from a hellhole and leaving you behind?

I caught the N Judah streetcar as usual at the Embarcadero underground station. I was feeling relieved, upbeat, and free. I looked forward to a pleasant, relaxing, and well-earned ride on the streetcar. I imagined celebrating with my ice-cold beer when I got home— maybe even two.

When we reached the Civic Center station, I was surprised to see Ben climb up from the stepwell at the front of the streetcar and deposit his coins into the farebox. I waved to him, motioning for him to come and sit beside me. He was as surprised as I was by our chance meeting.

He smiled as he made his way down the aisle, grabbing seat handles as the streetcar lurched forward.

When he dropped into the seat next to me, I asked where he was coming from. He said he had just spent a couple of hours at the San Francisco Public Library and that he had been going there each day for the past few days, researching Eastern meditation—especially kundalini yoga.

I told him this was my last ride home from Computer Connection and that I would be flying to St. Paul, Minnesota for two weeks of sales training on Sunday. He congratulated me and said he was very happy for me.

I asked how his yoga meditation was going and he said rather glumly that he hadn't been making the headway he had hoped—especially since his "sabbatical" was coming to an end. Still, he had some hope for a new approach he had just learned about at the library.

He spent the rest of the way home listening to me go on about how my life was about to change: how I would have a company car and a decent income, how I would have an expense account and a corporate business card, how I could get another suit—maybe even two new suits—how I would be able to save money, and how I might even be able to buy an Apple computer of my own someday. And so on and so on.

When we got back to our apartment building, I explained that I'd be spending Saturday packing and preparing for my flight on Sunday. After we said our goodbyes, he stepped into his apartment and I walked up the stairs to mine.

10   The Far in the Near

It was approaching sunset on Saturday when I finished eating my dinner. I had already finished packing and preparing for my flight to Minneapolis-St. Paul. I was just about to put my beer glass in the freezer when I heard a light knocking at my door. I opened it to see Ben standing there, smiling nervously.

"I thought someone should know," he said, "just in case."

There was anxiety in his eyes.

"I've done something to myself," he went on, "something to my body, and… well, I just don't know where it's going."

"Come in," I said, stepping back to let him in.

"Where should I go?" he asked, glancing left and right.

"Oh, that way, go that way," I said, pointing down the hallway.

He walked on, and I followed him into my living room.

"Have a seat," I said, gesturing to my easy chair.

"No thanks. I won't stay long," he replied politely.

"What's going on? Is everything okay?"

"Well, yes and no. I've caused something to happen—something that's stunned me. I'm in it right now and I think it may be wonderful. Well, it *is* wonderful. There's a golden shower—a warm silky liquid—showering down onto my brain. It's traveling up my spine. It's like my spinal cord is a pipe and it's streaming up through it. Like a garden hose with a nozzle lightly sprinkling nectar onto my brain. I'm not speaking metaphorically here. This is physically happening to me—right now.

I was dumbstruck by the flood of startling words pouring out of him.

He went on.

"If there's really such a thing as God's grace—this is it. It's like my brain is being continually anointed. I want this to go on forever—but then again, I just don't know. I don't know if I'll be able to do anything else. The infinite is all around me. I'm losing myself in everything I look at. It's wonderful, but I don't know if I will be able to concentrate on anything else. How will I be able to focus on my work— on teaching?"

"Well I don't—"

"There's so much *now* in me, there's no room for any future. How will I be able to focus on anything and accomplish anything? How will I be able to hold down a job? I want this, but I want to be able to control it. I want to be able to lose myself in infinity like this—but at *will*. I want to be able to turn it on and off—but what if I can't? I certainly can't do it right now. What if I've done something to my body and I'll be like this forever? Maybe I'll end up being a burden to people. I wouldn't want that— no, I wouldn't want that."

It was obvious from his words and his eyes that he was experiencing something big. His pupils were dilated. I'm sure a policeman would assume he was on drugs of some sort. If I didn't know that he was completely against taking drugs—even alcohol—I would have concluded that also. I was concerned for him, but curious too.

"What happened exactly? How did you bring this about?"

I don't think he heard my question. He was looking down at the backs of his hands. Then he turned them over and looked at his palms.

"I feel like I might be glowing. Do I look like I'm glowing?" he asked with childlike curiosity.

"It's hard to say," I said slowly. "It could just be the light coming from the window."

He turned his head and walked over to the window.

"So this is your window."

"Such as it is," I said indifferently.

"The light is wonderful on this side of the building."

"You think so?"

"Oh yes, it's a glorious light."

He stood looking out the window at an angle so he could see the pink-orange horizon in the direction of the ocean. He closed his eyes, letting himself bask in the light.

I never thought the light from my window, which faced the fire escape and a big tan building, was as glorious as he found it to be—not even at sunset. But I saw no point in contradicting him. I was more interested in finding out how he had gotten himself into his present state.

"Ben, how did all this happen? What exactly did you do?"

He opened his eyes and turned toward me.

"You know I've been meditating for some time now. I've had some remarkable experiences with it. There were times when I've managed to turn off my mind, to shut it down completely. Sometimes I felt as if I had broken out of time altogether. But I wanted more. I wanted cosmic consciousness, as you know."

He was looking at me, but not as he had so many times before, when his eyes seemed to penetrate me. Now they just seemed to behold me, like a child would.

"Anyway, in the San Francisco Public Library, I read about a technique used by those pursuing kundalini yoga where they lift themselves up from the lotus position—well, here, let me show you—"

Ben sat down on the floor and crossed his legs like yogis do.

"They press their hands to the floor like this, then they elevate themselves a little off the floor like this. Then they bang their butts down."

Ben lowered himself to the floor without actually completing the technique.

"I tried that just a few minutes ago. I had to do it a few times—and then suddenly—a jolt of warm liquid shot up my spine. It was as if semen was going up my spine. Now it's like my brain is having an orgasm."

"Right now?"

"Yes—right now."

"Maybe you did do something to your body," I said calmly, concealing my alarm. "Maybe you should see a doctor."

"No—no. I don't want to do that. What could a doctor do? How would he detect anything? I'm sure he would just refer me to a psychiatrist. No, let's see how this goes. I don't want to go public with this. Let's just keep this between us."

"All right," I said after a slight hesitation. "If that's what you want."

He seemed relieved. Just confiding in someone appeared to lift a burden from him, allowing him to give himself over to what he was experiencing—free of anxiety.

He stood up.

"This is so marvelous, Michael. There's nothing like it. It's rapture. Everywhere I look, I see infinity. If I look closely at something, it glitters. If I look at anything for a while, I lose myself in it. I tell you the joy is immense. It's ecstasy. This life is so wonderful. I don't need to look for enlightenment in books any longer. In fact, I don't think I could concentrate on a book. How could I? I would lose myself in the ink on the page… and then in the little microscopic chips of wood in the paper."

There was a faint smile on his face. I began to think his face did seem to have a glow to it, a kind of radiance.

"Let me ask you something," he asked with a shade of embarrassment, "do I have a halo around my head?"

"You mean a halo… like a saint would have?"

"Well, yes, but I don't mean to suggest that I'm especially good like a saint or anything. But do you see a glow of some sort around my head? Because that might explain what I'm feeling."

I did him the courtesy of looking closely at his head for a while. I even squinted.

"No, I can't say I see anything like a glow around your head."

"I think I need to go for a walk," he said suddenly. "Do you feel like a walk? I need to get outdoors."

I was concerned about him and the state he was in, so I didn't feel I could refuse him.

"Sure," I said. "I'm all packed and ready to go to my sales training. Besides, I didn't exercise today, so I need the exercise."

He walked toward the door and wandered out. I stayed back to get my keys and lock the door.

I caught up with Ben in the lobby. When we stepped outside our building, Ben stopped and breathed in deeply the pleasant early evening air through his nose. He let it out with a gratifying sigh. Instead of motioning to the left toward Golden Gate Park, he pointed to the right, and we started walking up 8th Avenue.

As we crossed over Judah Street, he asked me if I could feel the electricity radiating from the electric trolleybus's overhead power lines. I said I thought I heard a little hum, but didn't feel anything.

We continued up 8th Avenue, side by side. From time to time, I stole glances at him. He wasn't exactly smiling, but his eyes and facial muscles seemed like they were about to. His eyes were alert and open wider than normal. I could see the joy and ecstasy he said he was experiencing reflected in them.

"Oh look at that," he said, pointing to a red flowering gum tree on the other side of the street. "I need to look at that."

He crossed the street and I followed. He stepped close in to the small tree, peering closely at one of its red flowers.

"Look at this, Michael."

I stepped in and looked at the bright red flower he was pointing to. Its center reminded me of a yellow sun, surrounded by countless thin red filaments tipped with tiny white dots.

"Yes, very pretty," I said.

His face was full of amazement.

"Don't you see?"

I looked closely at the strange flower again.

"See what?"

"This."

He moved his fingers back and forth over the filaments with their tiny white dots without touching them.

"Yes, it's a wonderful flower. I don't think I ever paid much attention to them before. It's interesting that they have so many filaments instead of petals."

"No," he insisted. "Don't you see how it's radiating? It's emanating little showers of light—little packets of energy. Look how the spindles of light are jetting out, sprinkling softly like fireworks, and then disappearing into nothingness."

He again brushed his fingers near the filaments that sprang out around the flower's "sun."

"Look how those tiny showers of starlight become untouchable sprinkles of nothing."

I didn't know what to say.

"Really? If you say so."

We stood there for a few more moments. He kept looking down at the flower, enchanted and amazed. At one moment I thought I saw light from the flower reflecting off his face, but it was too brief for me to believe that it was anything more than my imagination.

"Shall we keep walking?" I suggested finally.

"Sure," he answered with agreeable absent-mindedness.

We walked away from the tree and returned to the sidewalk on the other side of 8th Avenue to continue up it. We crossed over Kirkham Street, Lawton Street, and then Moraga Street. It's steadily uphill, so I was beginning to feel the strain, though reminding myself that the exercise was good for me. Ben, however—even though he was a bit stockier than I was—seemed light on his feet. I don't think he even noticed he was walking uphill.

"It's very odd," he suddenly said, "it's as if my consciousness is slightly above the crown of my head."

"How do you mean?"

"Well, right now if you think about it, your consciousness—your focus of awareness—is right behind your eyes, isn't it?"

"Yes, I suppose it is."

"Well, with me, my consciousness is slightly above the crown of my head. The top back of my head."

He stopped walking and laid the palm of his hand on his head.

"This is considered the crown of the head, right?"

"Yes, I think so."

He raised his hand several inches away from his head.

"Well, this is where my consciousness is. It's hovering in this area. I feel as if I'm looking down on myself, from up and behind. My eyes are still my eyes. They still work. But the center of my consciousness is here—up here."

"You can still see?"

"Oh yes, perfectly! I can see things I've never been able to see before, on top of normal everyday things. Like that tree flower back there. If I look at things close up, it's as if my eyes have opened up a door to infinity—to the energy behind everything."

"So is that cosmic consciousness?"

"It has to be. I don't know what else it could be."

We started to walk again. We crossed over Noriega and Ortega Streets.

Further on, 8th Avenue turned into Pacheco Street as it entered the Forest Hills district. Here the street became more heavily tree-lined, and the homes were larger, richer, and architecturally distinct. Eventually we found ourselves at the traffic circle at the top of Claremont Boulevard. We crossed over it and began to walk down Claremont Boulevard itself. We had only walked a block when Ben put his hand on my shoulder.

"What's that?" He pointed to the left, down Granville Way, which was across the street from us.

"Oh, you mean at the end of that street? That's Mount Davidson."

"But what's that? That white thing, rising above the trees?"

"That's the cross."

"On top of the hill? It must be huge."

"Yes, I think it is. I've never been there myself."

"Let's go there. I want to see that."

"It's not as close as it looks. It's still quite a ways off."

"So what? You say you've never been there before. Don't you want to see it? Don't you want to go there?"

"Well, I guess I could use the exercise."

"That's the spirit."

We crossed over Claremont Boulevard and entered Granville Way. Ben walked in the center of the street, staring at the hill of green trees that seemed to be at the end of the street. The white top shaft of the cross and its white crossbeam were just visible above the curved treeline.

"We really should walk on the sidewalk," I cautioned.

"There aren't any cars coming, are there?"

"I know, but you never know. Don't worry, we'll be able to keep our goal in view most of the time. It's not going anywhere."

Ben nodded, and we angled over to the sidewalk.

"It's further than it looks," I reminded him.

"We can do it."

"I don't think it's at the end of this street. In fact, I'm not sure how to get there. Just to be clear, I've never been there before."

"I know. You already said that. We'll get there. We can't lose it now."

After walking down a few more curving streets, we eventually reached a set of steep red-brick stairs on Juanita Way. They rose up into a dark thicket of bushes, eucalyptus, and evergreen trees. We surmised that it had to be the way up to the top of Mount Davidson, so we started up them. The stairs led to a path that went in one direction and then turned sharply in the other. But since we were ascending, we concluded it must be leading us to the top. After feeling our way up different paths, we eventually came to an opening that from an airplane must have looked like a bald spot on top of a giant's head of hair. From there, we had a view of San Francisco, San Francisco Bay, and the cities of the East Bay.

"Look at the view Ben," I exclaimed. That's San Francisco in all its glory."

"Yes, very nice. Very impressive," he said indifferently.

"Look! That's Mount Sutro with its radio wave tower."

"How tall do you think that is?" he asked politely.

"I don't know. But as you can see, it's very tall.

"Yes, plainly."

We stood for a few more moments, taking in the view. Then Ben turned and looked back at the paths, obviously wondering which one would lead us to the cross.

"It's probably that one," I suggested, pointing to the path on the right.

We started up it. When we finally reached the cross we stood beneath it, marveling at its size and height—a gigantic, stark-white monolith with equally monolithic outstretched arms near the top. A colossal, skyscraping, elemental Christian symbol.

"How did this come to be here?" Ben asked.

"I don't know. But we really should be going," I said apprehensively. "The sun has already set. We don't want to be walking back down in the dark—it was hard enough getting up here with the light we had."

Ben agreed, and we made our way back down the paths to the brick stairs that brought us out to Juanita Way. Without the cross as our goal, I was uncertain which streets would take us back to the traffic circle at the top of Claremont Boulevard. Luckily, my sense of direction was good enough to get us there. When we crossed the traffic circle, I relaxed, confident in the way back to our apartment building from there.

We turned around to look at where we had come from— and saw something breathtaking. The huge yellow moon was hovering over Mount Davidson, and the cross stood as a black silhouette against it. We both gasped at the same time. I had never seen the moon so close to the Earth. From the way Ben was reacting, I could tell he hadn't either.

"If we had stayed up there, we could have touched that moon," he whispered.

The moonlight showed us the way through the sparsely street-lit Forest Hills neighborhood. When we were close to our apartment building, Ben crossed the street to look at his red flowering gum tree again.

"Those flowers are still little fountains of light," he announced happily when he came back.

When we crossed Judah Street, Ben asked again if I could feel the electricity of the electric trolleybus's overhead power lines.

"No, but I can hear a little hum," I replied.

11   Ben Disappears

On the flight back to San Francisco, I spent most of my time reflecting on the sales training I had just completed.

I was pleased to discover that there's real theory and methodology behind being a sales representative. Sales is a legitimate profession. Not at all like the stereotypical, aggressive, high-pressure sales tactics of used car salesmen that give the field a bad name. If a sales rep knows their product is genuinely good and valuable, their job is to find the people who need it and clearly explain its benefits. When you do that, you create in them the desire to buy your product or service. What could be wrong with that? And what could be wrong with making money by doing such a thing?

We had thick booklets with exercises on the many aspects of being a sales rep: product knowledge, prospecting, record keeping, order writing, and administrative tasks. Administrative duties included things like maintaining the company car, calling into the office once a day for messages, completing expense reports, and so on.

But for me, the most exciting part of the training consisted of the booklets that dealt with how to make actual sales calls. This included skills like building rapport, asking questions, responding to objections, and closing the sale. For me, that was the best part of the curriculum because it was all about human psychology and the power of persuasion.

We worked through all the booklets and training materials during many classroom hours that included lectures, discussions, exercises, and role-playing. It was like being in college again—only now I was getting paid to be there. At the same time, I was learning how to become a money-making professional.

In addition to the booklets and classroom activities, we had several guest speakers: retired sales reps who shared stories from their long careers in the field.

One old guy's advice was, "Don't ever corner a rat." If you catch a potential customer in a lie, don't accuse them of lying. Instead, turn it into a joke. Say something like: "Ha! Ha! I think you could sell me a bridge in Alaska—or maybe even one in Brooklyn!" Give the rat a way out. Give him a way to save face, and you still may be able to get his business.

Another sales veteran's insight was memorable too. He talked about greed and fear. Which of those two drives, he asked, is the strongest human motivator? He proposed a thought experiment: If you call someone in the middle of the night and tell them you know how they can make a thousand dollars, would they jump out of bed and take immediate action? No, probably not. But if you called them and said someone was breaking into their shed, wouldn't they would immediately jump out of bed to stop it? Why? Because the fear of losing something is the more powerful motivator. The desire to gain something—even greed—is simply not as strong. And isn't fear the basis for the entire insurance industry? And isn't it also the basis for much of any nation's foreign politics?

I stared at the back of the headrest of the seat in front of me, reflecting on all that I had discovered and experienced during my sales training. Then, for the first time since I had been away, I thought of Ben. I began to look forward to sharing with him everything I had learned and all the realizations I had come to.

It was then that pilot's voice came over the loudspeaker, saying we were approaching "Bagdad by the Bay." Just then, the plane must have hit turbulence, because it shuddered and lurched forward. In my mind, I suddenly saw Ben coming toward me, grabbing the seat handles on the N Judah streetcar as it lurched forward. At that moment I clearly remembered him telling me that his "sabbatical" was coming to an end. At the time, almost two weeks ago, I was too full of myself and too excited about my own life-changing events to pay close attention to what he was saying. Now, I realized that he was saying that he would soon be going back to his university for the start of the fall semester.

Suddenly, I had a sinking feeling that Ben wouldn't be there when I got back.

I spent the rest of the flight staring at the seatback in front of me, scolding myself for being so stupid and self-centered.

After we landed, I rushed out of the terminal to the Arrivals curb and caught the first blue shuttle bus I could find. I was on pins and needles when it pulled up in front of our building. Grabbing my suitcase, I scrambled out of the shuttle bus. With my key already in hand, I deftly unlocked the building's door. Soon I was gliding up the ten arabesque-tiled steps, past the shiny brown plaster lions, and rounding the corner to Ben's apartment. Anxiety made me knock on the door louder than I intended.

"Ben! Ben! Are you there?" I cried.

There was no reply, so I knocked again, harder this time.

The door on my left opened a sliver, then, after a pause, a full quarter. Half of Dorothy's face appeared. Her pink chiffon robe drifted partially out into the hall.

"He's not here Michael," she said coldly.

"He's not? Where is he?"

"He's gone."

"Gone where?"

"Back to where he came from."

"Where's that?"

"I don't know. Somewhere in the Midwest. And don't forget, your rent's due in a few days."

"Yes, I'm aware of that," I said as she closed her door.

I turned my head and stared at Ben's door, remembering the first time I had raised my hand to knock on it and the way door had suddenly flown open to reveal Ben standing there.

Sad and dejected, I reached down and picked up my suitcase. *I don't even know Ben's last name*, I thought to myself. *And I don't have a photograph of him, either.*

I turned away and slowly began to climb the stairs to the second floor. For a fleeting moment, I considered pausing on each step, as if that might somehow make Ben open his door and appear.

When I reached my door and opened it, I saw an envelope on the floor with my name on it. A thrill ran up my spine. I dropped my suitcase and picked up the envelope. I opened it and pulled out the letter.

Ben Backus and the Quest for Cosmic Consciousness

Greetings Michael!

A new semester is starting soon, so my "sabbatical" is over. But I go back with ideas for two new classes: Being and Identity *and* Philosophical Ideas in Literature. *I think I am uniquely qualified to be the instructor for both of those classes.*

But most important of all, there's a lovely woman back there waiting for an answer to a question she hasn't put into words. And now that I've achieved what I set out to do, I'm ready to give it to her.

Yes, I experienced the big realization of cosmic consciousness, and even though it's a fading force now, it's an experience I know I will have forever. I'm no longer worried whether I'll be able to focus and accomplish things in the everyday world. Eternity is going back to being an idea. Time is returning to its dominant position.

Four days after you left, I wandered into 9th Avenue Books and discovered a copy of Joseph Campbell's The Inner Reaches of Outer Space: Metaphor as Myth and as Religion. *The entire dust jacket was a photo of outer space: a myriad of white specks against a black background, with a purplish wisp of a nebula descending diagonally next to the title. I took it back to my apartment, and when I started to read it, I felt as if I were beholding an illuminated manuscript. Every word was a pool of meaning that I fell into. Every idea was wrapped in a halo of endless associations.*

Still, the joy I was feeling inside myself at that moment was more powerful than the words on the page before me. After a few paragraphs, I realized I couldn't summarize or recall anything I had just read. So I decided to try to write down what I was experiencing. But all I could manage to write was "Four days of" on the inside front cover. It seems that the ecstasy of cosmic consciousness—of supercharged being—produces few words. I couldn't, nor did I want to, express or write down what I was experiencing at that moment. Because how could I? That would only take my attention away from the joy—the bliss—I was experiencing. That's why the mystical experience is ineffable. That's why it's beyond words. If I turned away to try to express it, if I tried to focus my mind on it, I would, at that very moment, have to give up the joy and the ecstasy I was in.

But time has passed, and I can once again focus on daily tasks and think in straight lines if I want to. But even though I'm not experiencing cosmic consciousness, even though I'm not in it, the memory of having been there has made an indelible mark upon me and has transformed my being.

I know it will take time for me to realize all that I have learned. But for now, what I can say for sure is that the road to the spirit runs through the body. Feeling is first. Feeling is primary. Thoughts depend on feeling, our central nervous system, our unconscious. Yes, I identified with the universe—the cosmos—but I can also say that the universe identified with me. And what I now know, what I now feel, is that everything in the universe—including me—is at bottom one thing: energy, electricity, color, and light.

I wish you all the luck in the world Michael. I'm sure that one day you will find the right time to write your book.

Ben Backus

I shut the door. I walked over and sat down at my kitchen table. I laid Ben's letter down in front of me. I sat for a long time—how long, I don't know—staring into space, wondering what it would be like to experience what Ben had experienced.

Then I looked at the last part of the letter again, the part where he said I would find the time to write my book one day.

How did he know my secret? How did he know that I wanted to be a writer? How could he have seen that the source of my self-worth was that I was living with a secret pride in the present because I believed that—*in the future*—I would be a writer someday?

I wondered if I had let it slip out in some way during our conversations. But I could think of no time when I had said anything to him about my wanting to become a writer.

All those times he had stared so intently at me—perhaps he had seen it in the black holes in the center of my eyes.